The Haunting of Sea Scape House

CAT KNIGHT

Disclaimer

This story is a work of fiction, any resemblance to people is purely coincidence. All places, names, events, businesses, etc. are used in a fictional manner. All characters are from the imagination of the author.

Table of Contents

Table of Contents

PROGLOGUE

Harold stood on the cliff and looked down at the beach, fifty feet below. In the moonlight, the waves rolling in from the sea turned white as they washed over the sand. The sound of the surf met his ears, and he knew he had chosen the exact right spot. There was nothing like the sound of the sea to induce proper sleeping. He was of the opinion that the rhythmic arrival of the waves was seared into the human psyche.

Hadn't he read somewhere that human forebears had emerged from the oceans? Wasn't blood of the same salinity as the sea? Could there be a stronger tie? Harold wasn't sure, but it didn't matter. The manor house would have a perfect view, and when he finished with the steps cut into the cliff, there would be access to the beach, the waves. He closed his eyes and listened.

Yes, the steady beat of the waves would drown out the screams.

That was the real advantage of the location. Harold could continue his experiments, and unlike his house in the city, there would be no one to hear the screams that he so enjoyed. The manor house would be sufficiently isolated that he doubted any hikers would happen past. And any stroller on the beach would hear nothing but the surf and an occasional bird. That was encouraging. He would have privacy, and he dearly needed privacy. He took a last look at the sea and turned back to the excavation.

The house had been started. The basement had been dug. The earth floor would be covered with a stone floor in two days. The floor would be followed by stone walls. In no time, the basement would be finished. After that, the house would be erected, brick by brick.

The plans included his laboratory in the basement, where he would challenge science without fear. He knew that there were detractors in the world, people who would reject his theories and stop his science without a second thought. He meant to keep those people at bay. They were the naysayers. They had no idea how valuable his theories would be.

Harold walked back to the carriage, where his horse stood patiently. The horse was black like the carriage, a helpful colour as far as he was concerned. It slipped through the dark, as if it was made of night. Harold smiled at the thought. Could anyone fashion a carriage made of night? No, that was impossible. But it was a worthy consideration.

Harold opened the door and looked at the bundle, the bloodied sheet that was wrapped around Bridget? No, that name didn't sound right. Not Bridget, but Bethany?

No, that didn't sound right either. Not that it mattered. Her name was now "dead", as she was as dead as the earth where he would put her.

She hadn't been a big woman or an old woman, as Harold had no particular wish to experiment on the old and ugly. She had been a lonely woman, who had arrived from France in answer to an advertisement he had placed in a Paris paper. She wasn't an especially good worker, but she did possess a strong will that kept her alive longer than his usual specimen. He grabbed the bundle and shouldered it. She seemed heavier dead, but that could be scientifically proven impossible.

He carried Blanchette...yes, that was her name...to the excavation. There was a ladder that led to the bottom. Harold didn't want to risk the ladder, so he tossed her into the pit. He was pretty sure she wouldn't mind. He grabbed a shovel from the carriage and threw in the pit also. Then, he shed his coat and hat and climbed down. There was enough moonlight to work by. He grabbed the shovel and thought a moment. Where would he put her?

Not in the middle.

The stone masons would be particular about the middle. They would want that to be perfect, as it would be the first area that met the eye. No, a corner would do nicely for Blanchette. Shovel in hand, Harold selected a corner and went to work. The ground had already been prepared in a fashion. He had no problem digging out a reasonable grave. Then, he dragged the body to the hole and shoved her in. He regretted losing the sheet, but that couldn't be helped.

He consoled himself with the thought that the blood had ruined the sheet anyway. He was saving himself the trouble of setting it afire.

The coolness of the night chilled him, and he knew he had to finish. He piled in the dirt and tamped it down with the shovel. Then, he added a springling more of dirt to make the spot look like the rest of the pit. Satisfied, he climbed out of the pit and looked about.

All alone.

The sea soothed him.

He put on his coat and hat and took a last look at the corner where he had buried her. Was there a faint glow there? He blinked.

No glow, just his tired eyes.

With a smile, Harold returned to his carriage. The ride back to the city wouldn't take too long. With any luck, no one would spot him or ask a question. He would soon be safe in his house, ready for bed.

In a few months, when the manor house was finished, Harold would place another advertisement. Soon, another young woman with a yen for adventure in a foreign country would arrive at his doorstep. She wouldn't meet adventure. She would push the limits of science. Yes, she would serve a purpose far greater than herself. He would have to contain his enthusiasm for the moment.

For the moment.

CHAPTER ONE

Courtney stood at the edge of the cliff and stared out at the sea. The stiff breeze ruffled her long, red hair, which was a good thing, as far as she was concerned. Below, the waves crested and rolled onto the beach, the steady drumbeat that the North Sea always provided. The blue sky and bright sun were exactly right. The day was made for a sturdy chair, a thermos of tea, a thick blanket, and a good book. She could wile away the hours in the cool wind. Even as she considered it, a tern drifted past, floating on the breeze. She sometimes envied birds. They could go where they willed. She was stuck on the highways and byways. There always seemed to be a hedgerow blocking her way.

"Hello there."

Courtney turned. The man approaching her wore jeans and sturdy boots and a coat like hunters wore. Young, his brown, bushy beard might have hidden a handsome face. She couldn't tell. She had never been particularly fond of beards. They scratched.

"Hello," she replied. "Malcom, is it?"

"It is. You must be Courtney."

"That's me. Thank you for coming."

"Well, it's my job. This is the property?"

"It is. What do you think?"

"Well, we'll have to do a comprehensive survey. But you certainly have the breeze for some windmills."

"Not too many. I doubt my new neighbours would appreciate a huge wind farm."

"No, not that many, especially with the manor house there."

"Oh, the manor house is coming down. I can't very well leave it in the middle of the windmills."

"I agree. But it looks pretty good for its age. Are you sure you want to raze it?"

"I'm certain. But not before I take out everything of value. I've got to recover part of my investment right away. It's not like I'm rolling in money."

"Who is? Luckily, the push for more renewable energy is strong. We'll be looking for new places to invest in wind farms for the next decade."

"I certainly can't wait a decade. How long before I see some return?"

"Well, I have to complete the survey and then work up the plans. You're certain you're going to do away with the house?"

"It will be gone."

"That makes the planning a bit simpler. After that, we go to the government for all the proper permits and such. Once we have that, we can order the windmills and install the transmission equipment. There's no need for a windmill, if you can't send the energy somewhere."

"Exactly. So, with all the planning and the ordering and the installing, what are we talking about?"

"A year, I would suppose. Much of it depends on the availability of the equipment and supplies we'll need. Nothing seems to mesh these days, despite our best efforts."

"Is there any way to speed up the process?"

"I'm afraid not. Unless the winter is a harsh one, and people are freezing in their homes because there's not enough energy to go around."

"I certainly don't wish that. Well, I guess I can last a year, provided I can sell what's inside the house."

They looked at each other, and Courtney knew they had reached the end of the line, so to speak.

"Well, then, I'll be about my business," Malcom said. "I use a GPS surveying system that is highly accurate. So, I'll be able to build the plan in two or three weeks. It's all about situating the windmills for optimal power."

"Will you send me a copy of the plan?"

"Of course, I will keep you apprised every step of the way. We want our partners involved. By the way, I couldn't help but notice the steps running down the cliff. Do people use this beach?"

"Not so much anymore. I mean, I don't know about the old, old days, but the last two owners of the property committed suicide. No one is exactly sure why. One jumped off the cliff, which seems a bit much to me. The other was more traditional. He put a bullet in his head."

"I can certainly see why you're not planning on living here."

"Oh, but I will live here, while I'm gutting the place. I'm not about to waste petrol on commuting."

Malcom took a step back. "I admire that kind of courage."

"Save your admiration for the windmills you're going to install. The sooner, the better. Quid doesn't grow on trees."

Malcom nodded and headed away. Courtney watched, hoping beyond hope that the red tape would be overcome by necessity—hers. She turned from the house and walked back to the cliff. The wind blew her hair away from her face. In the distance, she spotted dark clouds. Was that an omen? Not for her.

Courtney was more than a little confident. She knew the manor house held treasures she could put on the market. She had enough savings to last—at least as long as it took to sell some things. She smiled. The manor house was a risk, but it was a manageable risk. Besides, she had a friend she could call upon to help put a value the antiques and even help to sell them. In fact, she needed to talk to Brianna right away. Brianna had offered to help. Good enough. Courtney pulled out her phone.

"I have a week."

Courtney looked across the table, as Brianna raised her glass of ale.

"Two weeks," Courtney said.

"You know I can't do two weeks, dear. Don't ask."

Brianna put down her glass and shook out her dark brown hair. Brianna was the woman all the blokes chased. She was flat pretty, with a figure that came straight from a bikini catalogue. Despite that, Brianna paid no attention to the blokes. She was waiting for a very rich, very handsome man. Brianna worked under the belief that she and Mr. Right would make beautiful babies that she could pamper. Courtney had no doubt that eventually Brianna would find her man.

"Ten days," Courtney said. "You can do ten days."

"You don't need me for ten days."

"Nonsense. Of course, I do. No one knows antiques like you do. I start putting things online without your help, and I'll lose my blouse."

Brianna frowned, a pretty frown. "Ten days. Not one day more. And on one condition. We do not argue about asking price. You list it for what I say, agreed?"

"A little bit of arguing?"

Brianna tilted her head to side.

"All right, you're the expert," Courtney said.

"When do we start?"

"Tomorrow?"

"The day after. And before I arrive, I want to know about the curse."

CHAPTER TWO

"What curse?" Courtney asked with a forced smile.

"The one that caused people to commit suicide."

"Oh, that curse. Well, as far as anyone knows there is no curse. Just some unstable people who couldn't cope with their lives. Happens every day, all over the world. This is no different."

"Please, Courtney, don't try to con me. I know a curse when I see one. There is something wrong with that house, and I want to know what it is."

"It doesn't matter, Bri. I'm going to tear down the house, remember? We're not going to live there. Ergo, no possible curse could pertain to us."

"Since when are curses stymied by living arrangements? We are going to sleep over, aren't we? I think that would qualify for the curse. So, are you going to tell me or what?"

Courtney thought a moment, wondering just how much background to reveal. It wasn't as if she knew all the details. And it really didn't matter. They weren't going to be in the house long enough to activate a curse of any kind.

"All right," Courtney said. "I don't know much about it, but it appears there was something wrong with the house at one time. The original builder was an odd duck, who liked to rove about the shire at night. Night owls are rarely celebrated. In any case, the man came to prominence when young women started disappearing. Ever since the Ripper, people get up in arms whenever something happens to young women. Men be damned, but a woman has to be protected. So, some of the locals approached the owner, demanding to see his basement, or dungeon, as they called it."

"And they found bones."

"No bones, but they found a sort of operating table. And some rather exotic restraints. That was all. The owner claimed he sometimes did experiments on animals. Purely for scientific purposes."

"But no one believed him?"

"Since they could prove nothing, they had to believe him. But some of the more rabid neighbours set up a watch. One night, they spotted the owner coming back from the city and followed him to the manor house. Sure enough, the man had a young woman, bound and gagged. That was enough for the neighbours, who confronted the man. He cursed them and everything else around...before he leaped from the cliff. He didn't survive."

"I should hope not. He was a monster."

"So, now you know."

"Does the man haunt the house? Does he invoke the curse against those who would dare to live there?"

"That is pure conjecture. No one has ever seen a ghost, and if there are some odd sounds and such, they're just the wind keening about the house. There's always a wind, and once the sun sets, the wind becomes a character in a horror movie."

"You will have TV and wi-fi, no?"

"Of course. How can we list items for sale, if we don't have access? You'll be able to surf to your heart's content."

"Good. That means I can call the Bobbies, whenever a ghost happens along."

"By the way, those two blokes who committed suicide were from the same family, a family known for mental defects. They were simply bonkers. No curse."

"You're not mentally defective, are you?"

Courtney laughed. "I am. This is my way of luring a pretty young woman into my lair."

"Don't make fun. Ghosts and curses are serious matters."

"You act as if you believe in such nonsense."

"Never let the dead know that you don't believe in them. That urges them to turn you into an acolyte. They can't rest, as long as there are doubters in their midst."

"Brianna, you've read too many Gothic novels. This house is not an old Scottish castle, filled with the screams from the dungeon. It's a manor house in poor repair, that will soon be replaced by giant windmills. The constant wind through the turbines will be the sound of money, my money. And that sound always drowns out the screams of the tortured."

"I don't know how you can be so blasé about the curse. Don't you believe in anything?"

"I believe that I have made a good investment that will pay handsomely in the near future. To believe in the nether world is to chase unicorns and fairies."

The waitress arrived with two pints. "From the bloke at the bar," the waitress said.

Courtney looked over, and the bloke raised his glass and smiled. Courtney smiled back, knowing that the smile would bring over the bloke, like a bone drew a pup.

"Don't look now," Courtney said, "but we're about to be invaded by blokes."

"Why is it that they think a pint entitles them to an hour or two of inane banter?"

"It's the nature of pubs. In fact, I think it's an unwritten rule. Or maybe, it's a written rule, one we don't get to read."

"Written on the same parchment that says they can tell the worst jokes imaginable and fart with a laugh."

"We should make up some rules and post them on the loo door. At least then, all the women would know what the rules are."

"I'll leave that to you," Brianna said. "You're the one with the imagination."

"Imagination, not belief. I can imagine ghosts. I am not going to believe in them."

"Hello, ladies," the bloke said, pint in hand. "Care for a chat?"

"Why not?" Brianna said and motioned at a chair.

The bloke sat and grinned, as if he had conquered Mt. Everest. "You're new here. I'm Clive, by the way."

Courtney looked at the man, whose brown beard was as thin as her pocketbook, which said something about him, something she didn't want to know. His brown eyes had been dulled by a pint or two, and his teeth begged for a straightening. His belly proclaimed his love of pints. His hands sported nails that needed a good washing. In short, he was the sort that the desperate encouraged. She was not desperate.

"I'm Allie," Brianna lied.

"I'm Zandra," Courtney added.

"Oooh, I like those names," he said. "What are you doing here?"

"Hunting ghosts," Brianna said.

"Finding any?"

"I think we happened upon the ghost of clever past," Courtney said. "I'm afraid the ghost of clever future will never arrive."

The bloke laughed. "I like that. Can I help?"

"Not tonight," Brianna said. "Here often?"

"Almost every night."

"Really?"

Courtney sipped her pint and wondered how long they needed to be polite. That was another rule that needed to be spelled out in black and white. Yes, a list of pub rules was needed badly. Of course, a list of "ghost" rules might be equally important—if there were any ghosts.

Courtney wondered just what it would take to make someone leap off a cliff. Then, she shook the notion out of her head. Why would she wonder about that?

CHAPTER THREE

Courtney stood on the gravel and stared at the manor house door. The fact that it was almost midday proved that she had had too many pints the night before. But she could hardly blame herself. The bloke kept bringing them to the table. How could she not drink them? Actually, Courtney didn't blame the bloke. She blamed Brianna who was the flame that drew the bloke-moths. The bloke-moths suffered the same fate as the real moths. Brianna-the-flame destroyed them.

"It doesn't look so bad," Brianna said. "For a haunted house."

"It's not haunted," Courtney said. "It is filled with antiques we can sell. Doesn't your head hurt?"

"Of course not. I don't drink like you. I sip. And I let the blokes finish for me. They get drunker, and I walk away half-sober."

"Why don't you share your clever tricks? I could have used that last night."

"We do have real beds, correct?" Brianna asked.

Courtney noticed the change of subject, but she didn't mind. Cancelling out the blokes and the beer seemed like a good idea.

"We have real beds and real heat, since I had the good sense to lay in a supply of logs. Fireplaces were the source of choice when this house was built."

"Then, let's get out of this wind."

Brianna marched for the door. Courtney followed for two steps and stopped.

"Bri," Courtney said.

"What?"

"Look at the third-floor window on the left. Is that a face?"

Brianna stopped and looked at the window. "I...I can't tell. It could be the light. No, no, it is a face."

Courtney laughed. "There's no face, ninny. I was just messing with you."

"That is not nice, Courtney. Remember the parable of the boy who cried 'wolf'."

"It wasn't a wolf."

"Don't be pedantic. If there is a ghost in there, you will definitely need my help."

With that, Brianna continued her march, leaving Courtney, who had the key, to catch up.

"It serves you right," Courtney said, as she unlocked the door. "You didn't give me your anti-bloke tips."

Courtney flicked on the lights and closed the door.

"This place must have been something in its day," Brianna said. "Even now, it has a certain elegance."

Courtney couldn't argue with Brianna. The entry was black and white, checkerboard marble. The chandelier was crystal. There was a coat rack and umbrella stand that drew Brianna's attention.

"I see what you mean," Brianna said. "These are antiques, and they appear to be in good condition."

Brianna pulled out her mobile and took pictures of the items. "I can't wait to look up comparable items for sale. You might have a gold mine here, Courtney."

"I need a gold mine," Courtney said. "Before you get into cataloguing the house, let's unpack. Third floor. Adjoining bedrooms."

"Separate loos?"

"Absolutely."

"What a holiday."

Brianna took the lead, even though she didn't know where she was going. That was Brianna. Courtney knew Brianna would lead. It was her nature.

The stairs were brown marble, and more than one riser was cracked. Courtney knew that was the problem with marble. It wasn't granite. Still, the steps were rich looking and not that worn.

"Marble will sell," Brianna noted. "Although we can't pull these out until we've sold off all the furniture. Have you arranged for a packing company to come in and crate items?"

"Not yet. I thought you might have a suggestion along that line."

"I do, and they're almost reasonable. Of course, shipping and handling will be added to the selling price."

"Of course."

At the top of the curving staircase, Courtney felt a draft of cold air.

"You have a leaky window," Brianna said. "I hope it's not in my room."

"I don't recall a leaky window, but that makes sense. After all, all the windows are old."

"If it gets too bad, we'll drape a blanket over it, or something. We're not going to repair windows at this stage."

Brianna's room became downright perky, after the lights came on. There was wood in the fireplace, ready for lighting. The windows faced the cliff and the sea, which sparkled in the sun.

"What a gorgeous view. No wonder the bloke built here. I bet people sat here for hours, staring at the sea, which is never quite the same one minute from the next."

Courtney shows Brianna the loo and the door that adjoined their rooms. Courtney's room was a twin, except for the décor. Where Brianna would sleep in azure blue, Courtney would have off-white.

"I'm thinking these rooms were reserved for betrothed couples," Brianna said. "With the door, they could arrange visits, without using the hall. Clever."

"Or it might have been parents and child. A mother could check on little Nancy without disturbing the household."

"Where is your sense of illicit love? These rooms were made for trysts, not bed checks."

"Speak for yourself. By the way, knock before you come in."

Brianna laughed. "Darling, I'm not coming through that door, unless you're screaming. And maybe, not even then."

They laughed. "Let's get the bags," Courtney said.

Courtney watched Brianna load up with bags.

"You're not moving in," Courtney said.

"You might pack like a schoolgirl traipsing through France, but I intend to recreate my city life. You don't intend to eat every meal in, do you?"

"Of course not," Courtney answered. "But I will wear the same outfit twice."

"And that's why you're still single."

"I'm single because I choose to be. How about you?"

"Because I haven't met a charming bloke who is swimming in money. I intend to love my husband, and I intend to live well."

Courtney grabbed one of Brianna's smaller bags and put the strap over her shoulder.

"Be careful with that one," Brianna said. "It's my laptop."

"I'll handle it with kid gloves."

"Just don't drop it."

Courtney added a second bag, to ease Brianna's load. Even so, Brianna looked like a bagboy at some fancy hotel.

"I don't think the queen travels with as many bags as you," Courtney said.

"The queen already has a rich husband."

"And servants."

Brianna looked up at the house. "I see him. I see your man."

"What?"

Courtney looked at the third-floor window. To her amazement, Brianna was right. A man looked down at them, and he did not look happy.

CHAPTER FOUR

"Oh, my god," Courtney said, even as the man disappeared from the window. "Come on."

"Come on?" Brianna asked.

"We have to get him out of there."

"That's a job for the Bobbies."

"Who knows where he'll be by the time the Bobbies get here. Come on. There are two of us, so we won't have any problem with that old man."

"You think he was old?"

"You're stalling." Courtney started for the door. "We need to do this."

"I'm coming," Brianna said. "But I wish to voice my opposition. We should wait for the Bobbies."

"If you're scared, we'll stop in the kitchen and grab knives."

"I'm scared."

Courtney tried the front door and found it locked.

"That's good," Brianna said. "He didn't come in through the front."

"We don't know that," Courtney said. "He might have locked it from the inside."

"Must you always rain on my parade? Now, you'll have me thinking he has a key."

"God forbid. I don't want to go to the trouble of changing the locks."

Courtney pushed the heavy door open and stepped into the entry. She heard Brianna enter and close the door.

"Lock it," Courtney said.

"What if we need to leave quickly?"

"What if the man has a partner?"

"Oh."

Courtney looked at the winding stairs, almost willing the man to appear. She heard Brianna lock the door.

"Third floor, correct?" Courtney asked.

"To the left," Brianna answered. "Kitchen first?"

"Absolutely. Go get knives. I'll watch the stairs."

"Whatever for?"

"Think of this as some sort of mouse hunt."

"This place has mice?"

"No...not that I know of. That's not the point. The point is that it's far easier to capture the mouse if it's confined to a single room. Chasing all about the house takes much more time and energy."

"I don't like mice, and I will leave if we spot a rat."

"No mice, no rats, not even a bug. Go, go, get the knives. We need to trap that old man."

Courtney watched Brianna walk off. Then, Courtney moved to the bottom of the staircase. She wasn't sure what she might do if the man bolted. She supposed she might try to stop him, but if he was bent on escape, all the better. Once he was gone, she could secure the house in any fashion she could devise, including propping chairs against the doors. That would not be a pretty sight, but it would serve the purpose. Anything that worked would be fine. It wasn't as if she was trying to save the house.

Brianna arrived with two long knives. Courtney accepted hers.

"Try not to cut me or yourself," Courtney said.

"I'm fully competent in knifing," Brianna said.

"'Knifing' is not a word."

"It is now. I'm right behind you."

Courtney laughed. "Why does that not surprise me?"

Courtney climbed the steps quickly. She had the sinking feeling that the old man was slipping away.

After all, she hadn't heard anything. A fleeing man had to make some noise in a squeaky, old house.

"I don't hear him," Brianna said, as if reading Courtney's mind.

"He's probably hiding under a bed or something. I don't imagine he wants to leave this comfy home."

"You know, we could just ignore him and go about our business. The wrecking crew will be here soon enough."

"Do you propose to sleep with that man running about the house? Want to take a shower? Sip wine by the fireplace?"

"You make him sound old and nasty. He might be just some homeless person who is kind and sweet on the inside."

"Did he look kind and sweet?"

Courtney reached the third floor and pointed. "That way?"

"I believe so."

Knowing that Brianna would not lead, Courtney marched down the hall. Her steps raised little clouds of dust that were barely visible against the dark pattern of the carpet. No wonder, she hadn't heard the interloper. Only a rhino would make a sound on the carpet.

"Someone needs to vacuum," Brianna said.

"No reason."

"I have a touch of asthma. This dust and dander and who knows what sort of insect leavings might trigger an attack."

"You have an inhaler for that. So, keep up. If you find that you can't breathe, you can leave."

"You need to think of someone besides yourself. I have a delicate disposition."

Courtney reached the last room and found the door closed.

"Here we go," Courtney said. "Keep your wits about you. I'll do the talking."

"I'll do the knifing."

"Exactly."

Courtney turned the old, glass knob and pushed open the door.

"Explain yourself," Courtney said, as she entered.

No one answered.

She looked about the bedroom, with its dated bed, still under its brocade cover.

"Is he there?" Brianna asked.

"No, well, not that I can see."

Trepidation quivered inside Courtney. She had expected the man to be there. Feisty, perhaps, but certainly visible.

"It will do no good to hide," Courtney called out. "So, let's be adults about this. Show yourself."

No one appeared, and the fear inside Courtney rooted itself. Cold, it sank tendrils into her body and mind. Where was he?

"I'm going to check the closet," Courtney said. "Look under the bed."

"I think I should guard the door," Brianna said. "You know, in case, he tries to escape."

"You don't have to crawl under the bed. Just get down on hands and knees and look."

"I have asthma, and I bet it's been decades since this carpet was cleaned."

Courtney looked about, at the antique bed, the dark blue, wingback chairs, the round oak table with its period lamp and layer of dust. The fireplace looked as if it hadn't seen a fire since the middle of the last century.

"All right, guard the door," Courtney said. "I'll look."

Courtney dropped to her knees, raising yet one more puff of dust. She looked under the bed and saw a...face, a mean, angry face.

Courtney immediately popped up, unable to even speak.

"What?" Brianna asked.

Courtney pointed under the bed.

"What?" Brianna repeated.

Courtney rolled her eyes and pointed again.

"Whatever," Brianna said and dropped to the carpet. She looked under the bed from five feet away. "What? I don't see anything."

"What?" Courtney said and looked again.

The face was gone.

"I...I saw him," Courtney said.

"Under the bed?"

"Yes, a man, well, the face of a man."

"Not the whole man?"

"I didn't look long enough."

"He's gone now. Are you sure?"

"I know what I saw." Courtney took another look. Nothing. She shivered. The face had been so...real.

"I'll check the closet," Courtney said.

"If you see a face, ask if there's a leaky window."

"Very funny."

The closet was empty except for some boxes on the shelves. She would have to examine the boxes, but that would come later. For the moment, she was content to accept that the man wasn't there.

The loo was small, and while the house had water, this loo did not. And there was no shower curtain to hide behind, as there was no shower. Courtney opened the narrow linen closet. Two dusty towels occupied a shelf. The towels were slated for the trash bin.

"He's not here," Courtney said as she left the loo.

"Well, that makes sense," Brianna said. "He saw us and ran."

"We have to search the house."

Brianna frowned. "I suppose you're right. I would hate to be murdered in my sleep."

"You won't be murdered in your sleep."

"Not if we find him and eject him from the house."

"Which we will."

They walked into the hall, and Courtney closed the door to the bedroom.

"What if the bloke isn't really a bloke? What if it's a ghost, a mean ghost?"

"No ghost. Just a bloke. You'll see."

"I don't like this, not one little bit."

"We just need to find him."

Courtney looked at Brianna, whose eyes darted about, like a cornered animal.

"Which way?" Brianna asked.

"We work our way back to the stairs and then down the other side."

"We start with this little door?"

"It would appear so."

Courtney opened the narrow door and found a set of narrow stairs.

"What is it?" Brianna asked.

"The attic."

CHAPTER FIVE

"I'll wait down here," Brianna said.

"No, you won't." Courtney put a bit of steel in her voice. "I'm guessing he's up there, since he didn't come down. So, we go together. I'll lead."

"Is it dark?"

"I'm hoping the attic can be lit, but if not, I believe it has several dormers that will give us light."

"I don't like this."

Courtney marched up the steps, her mouth dry and her hand shaky. The icy fear was growing, filling her brain. What if the man was in the attic? What if he put up a fight? Why hadn't she taken Brianna's advice and called the Bobbies? She reached the top and took a deep breath. Then, she stepped into the attic and looked for a light switch.

Which she didn't find.

The darkness of the attic was not complete. As anticipated, several dormers fed light into the shadowy gloom. To Courtney, the room was twilight, that time between light and dark, when shadows crept from under trees and banded together to spread fear. There were no trees in the attic, but the long room was filled with the flotsam and jetsam of life.

Trunks, lamps without shades, boxes, several broken chairs meant for repair, the room was the shore of the house, accepting the castoffs. She looked around, half expecting the old man to be leering at her. She didn't spot him.

"Is he there?" Brianna asked.

"I don't see him," Courtney said. "Guard the stairs while I take a better look."

"Do I have to?"

"Yes."

"And if he wants out?"

"You're the knifer, right?"

Courtney sniffed the air. Was there a hint of something dead, something dying, something decaying? It wasn't a stench. It was more like an aftermath, after the thing had died and mostly disappeared. No flies, no maggots, just a skeleton perhaps with a leathery layer of ancient skin.

She remembered that when she was young, her little brother brought home a chameleon. He kept it in an aquarium, and it was fun to change the lizard's background and watch its skin turn colour. One day, they came home from school and found the aquarium empty.

They searched the entire house, but they couldn't find it. She guessed that somehow the little thing had managed to slip under a door and escape to the garden. No doubt it became a tasty treat for some hawk or snake. It wasn't until the fridge died that they discovered the chameleon's carcass, what was left of it. Dry, empty, what might have passed for a dinosaur remnant. She thought that if she moved enough boxes and trunks, she would find a mouse in the same desiccated condition.

A hint of death.

Courtney walked the length of the attic, looking high and low through the shadows. Every time she peeked around a box, she expected the man to leap out and shout BOO! Of course, nothing like that happened. She reached the end and turned back. Then, she stopped.

The doorway was empty. No Brianna, no knife, nothing but a dark hole, like a cave. What had happened to Brianna?

Courtney's first thought was that the man had come back and grabbed Brianna, stifled her before she could utter a word of warning. Even as Courtney stood frozen, the man was dragging Brianna down the stairs, perhaps to the basement, the dungeon as some of the locals called it.

"Brianna," Courtney said.

No answer.

Courtney took a step toward the doorway and stopped. She squinted into the shadows. Was there a knife on the dusty floor?

Had Brianna dropped it in the struggle? Did it gleam right before her? She tilted her head to the side, changing the angle. Was it...?

No, there was no knife on the floor.

"Brianna."

No answer.

Courtney gripped and regripped her knife. She slid her feet along the floor, afraid to lift them and make some noise that would tell the old man where she was. Her hand shook, the knife vibrating up and down, like some sort of tuning fork. Did she hear something? She stopped. Was it a gasp? Was it a gagged scream?

"Brianna."

No answer.

Courtney knew that the longer she hesitated, the better chance that Brianna had come to harm. The ice fear gripped her brain, her thoughts. She found herself unable to move, petrified. Yet, she had to move. She ground her teeth and stumbled forward, heading for the door, the stairs.

At the top of the stairs, Courtney stopped.

"Brianna."

No answer.

Courtney pounded down the steps, no longer heeding caution. She had to get away from the attic. She had to find Brianna, before the man did something awful. Why had she turned her back on Brianna? Why hadn't she been more aware? Now, she faced a wicked task.

She had to find Brianna before the homeless man turned Brianna's knife against her. Courtney lurched into the hall.

"BRIANNA!"

No answer.

Panic ballooned inside her head. Courtney stumbled down the hall. Finding Brianna before she became some sort of bloody puppet was Courtney's only thought. She could feel the evil all about her. She could almost hear the guttural voice mocking Brianna, promising pain, assuring her that no rescue was coming.

Courtney reached the top of the stairs. Her heart pounded. The drumbeat in her ears was deafening. She grabbed the railing with one hand and started down.

"BRIANNA!"

"What do you want?"

Courtney stopped and turned.

At the top of the stairs, Brianna frowned. "What do you want?"

"Where were you?"

"I had to use the loo."

"Why didn't you tell me?"

"I did."

Courtney blinked and shook her head. "You did?"

"Yes, and I might have waited around for an answer, but you were too busy. And I had to go."

Courtney tried to remember. Had she been so engrossed that she missed Brianna's words? That seem possible, but Courtney didn't believe it for a moment. Something in the attic had stopped Brianna's voice. Something wanted Courtney to panic. Something lived for the fear that exploded inside Courtney's head.

Something.

"I need a drink," Courtney said.

"Now, that is a good idea," Brianna said.

Courtney turned and started down, only to be stopped by the...

CACKLE.

CHAPTER SIX

"What the bloody hell was that?" Brianna asked.

"That was our visitor," Courtney answered. "Not pleasant, is he?"

"That's downright scary. Where did it come from?"

"I don't know. But I need that bloody drink. Come along."

Courtney led the way to the kitchen, which did not show the signs of decay that the third floor had evidenced. She didn't bother looking over her shoulder. She knew Brianna was following.

The kitchen had been modernized to a certain extent. The fridge and stove worked. The water flowed. With its table and chairs, it was a comfy place. That it felt chilly to Courtney didn't bother her. She would be warmed up soon enough. She went to the pantry, which had supplies for the two weeks Courtney thought they needed to get the saleable things out the door.

"What would you like?" Courtney asked. "Wine or vodka?"

"It's too early for wine, and I need a jolt. Vodka, rocks."

"You got it."

Five minutes later, Courtney delivered vodka and ice in a tall, cut crystal glass.

"Elegant," Brianna said.

"It came with the house. There's an entire set of tumblers and glasses, even a pitcher. What's the set worth?"

"Oh, I would guess a hundred quid, depending on what my research uncovers. You can never know with crystal like this. Find the right buyer, and it fetches a pretty pence."

Courtney poured herself a drink and arrived at the table with a bag of crisps.

"Ahh," Brianna said. "Original crisps, my favourite. I don't fancy all the flavours they have these days. Who wants an onion crisp?"

"Agreed." Courtney opened the package before she held up her glass. "To getting the stranger out of my house."

"I'll drink to that."

The vodka tasted a bit harsh. That was fine with Courtney. She needed to feel something besides fear. If liquid courage sufficed, she and Brianna would soon be rid of the nuisance.

"How do you propose to get rid of him?" Brianna asked.

"I was thinking on that," Courtney said. "We could do a top to bottom or bottom to top search, but this is a big, old house. He might know of a priest's hole or a cupboard that we might overlook. We might never find him."

"But we have to find him. I don't see how we can stay here, with him in the house."

"That would seem to be a bad strategy, but it's not impossible. Think about it. So far, the man has been little more than a blip on our radar. He means to scare us into leaving. We don't have to. Besides, if we wait, I have the feeling he will reveal himself. He can't abide us being here."

"That makes a certain sense. But I have no desire to be murdered in my sleep."

"Don't be so dramatic," Courtney said. "We'll lock and barricade the doors, so he can't get in. That will frustrate him to the point that he'll make a mistake, and we'll grab him."

Brianna tapped her nose with a crisp. "Shouldn't we bring in the police? They could probably search better than you and me."

"They might, and they might not. They might tell us to call them once we have the bloke cornered or something. You know the Bobbies. They're not as dependable, as they once were."

"I suppose that if they came and found nothing, they wouldn't come a second time, no matter what we screamed at them."

"The girls who cried wolf."

"If I understand you correctly, you're proposing that we go about our business, as if we were all alone. If the bloke shows himself, we whack him with a cricket bat or something. If he doesn't, it doesn't matter. We'll strip the place, and the wrecking ball will send him packing."

Courtney nodded and ate a crisp. "I'm not saying it won't be taxing. The bloke has the advantage, as he can try to scare us whenever he feels the need. But, as long as we keep our heads, we can ignore him. And with all the coming and going of shipping trucks, he'll have to hide most of the time."

"You make it sound so rational," Brianna said. "Just pack away a lamp and pat the bloke on the forehead. What happens if he doesn't take the hint?"

"We will still have the Bobbies. And if we can actually capture him, or confine him to a particular room, then they can take him away."

"You're not afraid?"

Courtney thought a moment. "I am afraid. After all, he might have a cricket bat himself. So, we must be alert and have our knives ready. And we should stick together as much as possible. It is a fact that there is safety in numbers."

"Make sure we know where the other is all the time?"

"If we propose to continue our tasks and ignore him."

"You do know that this is not what would happen in one of those made-for-telly movies. In those, we would spend the next three days hunting down this ghost."

"Yes, and acting silly. You know, crying and carrying on, afraid of our own shadows. I swear, those movies make everyone appear like a ninny. There is no reason to lose your head. We know what we're facing. We can manage it."

Brianna smiled. "All right, then, we will muddle through and ignore the bloke, until such time that we can grab him and tie him into a nice, neat package for the Bobbies."

"Let him come to us," Courtney said. "We'll deal with him then."

"If he doesn't come to us?"

"So much the better. We will be able to work in peace." Courtney picked up her knife and looked at the sharp blade. "We won't hurt him unless we have to, agreed?"

"Agreed. Should we sleep in the same room?"

"I don't believe that is necessary. However, should he prove a real spanner, we can always move in together. Another drink?"

"Another drink was exactly what I was thinking," Brianna said. "We'll discuss where we should start. I'm guessing, we need to take photos of the art on the walls and do some research."

"Piecemeal sales, or as a collection?"

"A collection, I would think. But we'll figure that out when we approach the auction houses."

Courtney made them second drinks. She had just taken her seat, when it came a second time...

CACKLE.

CHAPTER SEVEN

Courtney shivered, as the cackle slowly dissipated, as if sustained by some blast of unholy air.

"I wish I had a gun," Brianna said.

"Have you ever fired a gun?" Courtney asked.

"No, but how hard can it be? I mean, in all the movies, it's just pick up, aim, and pull the trigger. Pretty, bloody simple."

"Everything is in the movies. I think it requires a bit of practice if you actually intend to hit something. Preferably, something you intend to hit."

"I'm betting I wouldn't have to shoot the gun at all. I could just wave it and scare the bloke to death." Brianna pointed a finger and waved it in the air.

"A gun in your hands would sure scare the hell out of me."

"Cute. You don't think he'll cackle all night, do you?"

"Not a chance. He means to scare us and get us to leave. After all, we have invaded his space.

If you look at it from his point of view." Courtney tilted her head to one side, as if looking afresh.

"Then, the sooner we start what we came to do, the better off we'll be. We simply have to ignore his childish efforts to scare us."

"I agree. Let's finish these drinks and get to work. Where would you like to start?"

"We should put it into some sort of order. Going at it willy-nilly ensures failure...in my mind."

"Top to bottom, or bottom to top? You'll have to bring your phone, so you can take pics."

"Let's skip the attic for the moment. How about the bedrooms? I'm sure there's some art in those."

"Agreed. Let's start on the third floor. Take pics, catalogue them by floor and room, so we can find them when we need them."

"Works for me." Brianna tossed down her drink and pushed herself from the table. "You know, if he has nothing more than that bloody cackle, then we'll have him out in a thrice."

"A thrice?"

"You know, quickly."

Courtney finished her drink and took the glasses to the sink.

"You'll mix them up," Brianna said.

"We'll get fresh ones for the next round."

"We still have to wash them."

Courtney shook her head. "The dishwasher will do nicely."

"You don't put fine crystal in a dishwasher," Brianna said. "Hand wash only."

"You're no fun."

"Agreed. Let's go."

Courtney and Brianna had reached the doorway, when the first glass whizzed past and shattered on the wall.

For a moment, neither woman could react. The shattered glass was so surprising it left them speechless. Courtney was trying to find her wits, when the second glass smashed close to the first. This time, a piece of glass whipped across Brianna's arm.

"Ouch," Brianna said.

The sound of Brianna's voice gave Courtney enough energy to turn. She expected to see the bloke at the sink, smirking or perhaps getting ready to hurl something else. Instead, she saw nothing. No one. She frowned. Where had he gone? He hardly had time enough to run out the door.

"I'm cut," Brianna said. "I'm bloody cut."

Courtney looked over. Brianna brandished her arm. She was cut, but to Courtney's eye, it wasn't much of a cut, more like a scratch. Still, it was bleeding. That was something.

"Where did he go?" Brianna asked.

"I don't know," Courtney answered. "He just vanished."

"Blokes don't just vanish. Let's find the bloody piker and teach him a lesson he'll never forget."

"We have to fix your arm first," Courtney said. "Otherwise, you'll be bleeding all over my valuable antiques."

"Give me a break. We have yet to find a valuable antique, and your crystal set just lost two of its members."

"I'll have the bloke's balls for that."

"I don't suppose you brought a first aid kit," Brianna said.

"No, but I did lay in a supply of bandages and such. I thought it wise, as we would be working with all sorts of things."

"Lead on, then."

"Have a seat. The supplies are in my bedroom. I'll be right back."

"Before you leave? Fetch me another vodka?"

Courtney chuckled. "You never miss a chance for a drink, do you?"

"My dear, drinking is a lost art, that I intend to resurrect. Don't skimp on the vodka."

"If the bloke returns," Courtney said. "Scream. I'll come running. He won't be able to hurt both of us."

"He's not exactly a great thrower, is he?"

Courtney pulled an everyday glass from a cabinet and fixed Brianna's drink. Courtney added two paper napkins, one for the glass and one for her arm.

"Don't bleed to death," Courtney said.

"What if the bloke isn't real?" Brianna asked.

"Isn't real?"

"What if it's a ghost? That's why we can't find him. That's why we didn't see anyone throw glasses. That's why we hear that...laugh."

"There are no ghosts, Brianna. None. Nada. Zip. Zilch."

"But what if there are? What if one is here?"

A cold wave flowed through Courtney's chest. She fought the urge to run.

"If...if there is a ghost," Courtney said. "Then, we'll deal with it."

"How can you deal with a ghost?"

"I don't know for certain, but we'll do it."

Brianna's face screwed up, as if she were about to cry. "I don't like ghosts."

"Don't think about it. Do you want first aid or not?"

"Just hurry. The sooner we treat the cut, the better it will be. The last thing I need is an infection."

Courtney grabbed her knife and marched out of the kitchen. She was pretty sure; it was the sight of the knives that made the bloke throw glasses instead of attacking in some other fashion. On the way to her bedroom, Courtney was careful to keep her eyes up, with frequent glances behind. The bloke had proved himself a coward, by throwing glasses from behind. That meant he was not above a sneak attack.

She would be ready for him. Although, she was not at all certain she could stab a person. That seemed so extreme.

Her bedroom was empty, as she expected. She hurried to the closet and pulled down the small, red bag from the shelf. It was red because that was the universal colour of the Red Cross. She had picked the colour on purpose, and she felt rather proud of that. Holding the bag in one hand and the knife in the other, she reversed her steps. She expected a cackle as she descended to the kitchen. She was vigilant all the way to the kitchen doorway. In fact, she was super vigilant, which made her stop as soon as she entered.

The table was empty.

Brianna was gone.

The glass was still there.

Courtney shook her head. When was Brianna going to learn to say something when she disappeared into the loo? With a bloke in the house, it made no sense to just run off.

Courtney set the bag on the table and looked about. She thought, perhaps, that she might take a loo break also.

That was before the lights winked out.

CHAPTER EIGHT

CACKLE.

A chill raced up Courtney's spine. She froze, standing by the table in the near dark. She couldn't think. Where was Brianna? How had he killed the lights? Were they out all over the house or just in the kitchen? The main panel was in the basement— she thought it was. Hadn't the electrician said that? Could she find it? While there was some light in the kitchen, the basement would be jet black, right? No windows in the dungeon. Nothing but a darkness that smelled faintly of death. She shivered afresh.

She wasn't about to go into the dungeon, not alone, not without a torch. No doubt, the bloke knew the dungeon forward and backward. He was the head torturer, or whatever he might be called. Bloody hell, she needed a gun. Why hadn't she thought of that? Primarily, because guns were almost impossible to acquire. Bloody, bloody hell.

"BRIANNA!" Courtney yelled, listening to the faint echo, as her voice moved through the house.

For some reason, her voice didn't sound nearly as loud as the cackle. Why was that? It didn't seem right. What was even more wrong was that Brianna had not answered. Surely, she had heard. Courtney had yelled loud enough to wake the dead, as her mother used to say.

Courtney thought about that for a moment. Did those who held vigil at the side of the dead actually shout at them? Were they trying to wake the dead by noise? That didn't seem possible, but she supposed anything might have happened in the days before deaths were certified.

As her eyes adjusted to the light, she noticed Brianna's drink was still half-full. That was enough for Courtney. She grabbed the glass and downed what was left. The vodka left a trail of heat through her chest. That was a good thing. The heat melted the ice in her spine. She felt herself again—almost. Putting down the glass, she decided she needed to take some initiative.

"WHOEVER YOU ARE," Courtney called. "YOU HAD BETTER RUN. RIGHT NOW! BECAUSE YOU ARE A TRESPASSER! AND I DEAL HARSHLY WITH TRESPASSERS. YOU WILL BE ACCOSTED BEFORE YOU ARE TURNED OVER TO THE BOBBIES! AND I WILL PRESS CHARGES TO THE HILT! HEAR ME?! TO THE BLOODY HILT!"

Courtney spotted the fork just before it buried its tines in her arm.

Courtney's SCREAM tore from her throat, even as she jerked the bloody fork from her arm. Pain rushed up her arm. She hurled the fork across the kitchen and grabbed arm, trying to gauge the wound by the amount of blood she could feel.

There wasn't much blood. Puncture wounds didn't bleed overmuch, did they? Wasn't that the problem? Weren't wounds supposed to bleed a little? To clear away any nasty germs? Hadn't she heard that somewhere?

She stared at her arm, trying to discern the damage. She felt the little holes in her arm. Definitely blood, not much. She wanted to scream. What was the bloke doing?

A fork?

"BLOODY SOD," she shouted. "YOU WILL PAY FOR THIS!" She grabbed her knife. "I WILL FIND YOU. BRIANNA!"

Courtney slipped her foot ahead, able to see enough, although not enough. She was almost certain she had brought a torch with her. Where had she placed it? She knew, knew it was in the kitchen, because everything was in the kitchen. She had done that purposefully. There was no need to spread things about the manor house. She wouldn't be staying that long.

Which drawer?

She reached for the cabinets, and something brushed across the back of her neck.

"EEEK"

Courtney spun, slashing with the knife, even as she did. Her blade found nothing. She slashed again, certain that the bloke had been right behind her. How else could he have touched her?

"PIG! WHERE ARE YOU?"

CACKLE

The voice was to one side, and not close, not close at all, which wasn't possible. She turned to the voice.

"Where is Brianna?" Courtney asked. "What have you done with her?" She moved slowly into the darkness near the pantry.

Pantry.

She had left the torch in the pantry. She was certain of that. Once she had the torch, she would be able to see the cad. It was only as she neared the shadowed corner that she felt a tinge of fear. Something about the bloke wasn't right, but she couldn't quite put her finger on it. Yet, it frightened her.

She was reminded of the chap they called the Ripper. He had been more than a bit off, hadn't he? Slicing and dicing women in the dark? Was the bloke like the Ripper? Was the bloke toying until he decided to strike.

"Bloody hell," she said. "I'm coming for you. I'm coming."

Courtney reached the pantry and grabbed the doorknob. Her arm ached from the puncture wounds, and, although she knew the bloke couldn't be close, she *felt* him. It was a tiny tingle along her neck, her arm, her skin. He was touching her all over, and yet, he wasn't touching her at all. It was as if she was a child again, rolling about in the grass. Then, standing and discovering her skin alight with itty-bitty fires, all over, as if she had been bitten by a million tiny gnats or midges or whatever. She wanted to scratch herself all over.

And she hadn't been rolling in the grass.

She pulled open the door and faced an impenetrable blackness. No light bled into the room. It was a void that she did not want to enter.

She scratched her skin without really knowing it. The puncture wounds had begun to throb. A voice way back inside her head spoke to her. It was a whisper. She had to strain to hear it. But she didn't have to hear it. The voice told her to run, to get out of the manor house as quickly as possible. What waited for her was a bloke she could not overcome. She had to...run.

Courtney gaped at the dark. Her knees shook. The knife bobbed up and down in her hand. The torch was there, there. All she had to do was step inside and feel around. Certainly, she could do that.

Her skin crawled.

She raked her nails across the puncture wounds.

"Double bloody hell," she whispered.

She stepped into the absolute dark and...tripped, slamming her shoulder on the wooden floor.

Courtney moaned.

The person she had tripped over moaned too.

CHAPTER NINE

"Brianna?" Courtney asked softly.

The moan that answered wasn't exactly what Courtney was looking for, but she would take it for a yes. Carefully, Courtney reached out and felt Brianna's...arm.

"Are you bleeding?" Courtney asked. "I mean, besides your arm. Can you talk."

"My head," Brianna said brokenly. "Something hit me in the head."

"Hold still. I'll check you out. Don't move. If you have a concussion, you could cause a real problem."

"Like...like this one isn't enough?"

Courtney walked her hand up Brianna's arm, all the way to her neck. Then, she slowly examined Brianna's head.

"Did you see who hit you?" Courtney asked.

"No. I don't remember getting here. I was sitting...ow."

"Sorry. You have a lump, but I don't feel any blood. He knocked you out?"

"Y...yes. I don't know how. I didn't see or hear him."

"He got me too. With a fork. He threw it, and it stuck in my arm."

"A fork? That's...unusual."

"Yeah, but I'm glad I tripped over you."

Brianna's laugh was cut short by a moan. "Don't make me laugh. It hurts too much."

"I won't. But you're lucky. The only reason I came in here was to fetch the torch. I'm sure it's in here somewhere."

"How do you hope to find it? I can't see anything."

"The same way I found you. I'll blunder into it. Do you think you can stand?"

"In a minute or two. The beginnings of a pounding headache are finding root in my brain."

"I brought pain killer. It's in the first-aid bag on the table. As soon as I find the torch, we'll take care of you."

"In that case, have at it. I need to take something quickly, before the headache becomes a full-blown storm."

"Lie still. And don't trip me."

Brianna chuckled.

Courtney grabbed one of the low shelves and started to pull herself up, only to pant with pain. Her shoulder didn't want to work.

"What is it?" Brianna asked.

"You're not the only one who needs some pain mitigation. I landed on my shoulder, and now, it doesn't care to work."

"Take your time. If you conk out, we'll really be in bad shape."

Courtney switched arms and slowly raised herself. "I wonder why he didn't hurt you worse."

"You're upset because he didn't gut me like some pig?"

"No, no, you know better. But he had the chance to really harm you, and yet he didn't."

"Torch, Courtney. Find the torch, before he overhears you and decides you're making sense."

On her feet, Courtney held the knife in one hand and slowly played her fingers over the shelves, which were mostly empty.

"You know," Courtney said. "I was lucky not to cut myself with this stupid knife."

"I seem to have dropped mine."

"No mind. We'll get you another."

Courtney's fingers found the torch. "Ah ha! Success."

Even as she grabbed the torch, the lights winked on in the kitchen. Brightness flowed into the pantry.

"That is one very powerful torch," Brianna said.

"Hush," Courtney said. "That wasn't right."

"What's not right about the bloody light?"

"The way it came on when I found the torch."

"And that bothers you?"

"It was completely dark, which means the bloke couldn't see me, couldn't know I had found the torch."

"You announced it, remember?"

"Yes, but he couldn't have reacted so quickly. That isn't possible."

"Then, it was coincident. Help me up."

Courtney pulled the torch off the shelf and turned it on.

"We don't need it now," Brianna said.

"We will if he kills the lights again." She handed the torch to Brianna. "Hold onto it."

"Upon my life."

"Don't get dramatic."

Courtney laid her knife on a shelf and grabbed the hand Brianna offered. It took some doing, but in a few seconds and with a modicum of pain, Brianna was off the floor. She leaned into Courtney.

"Steady me for a few seconds," Brianna said. "I'm a bit woozy."

Courtney wrapped an arm around Brianna's waist. "You know," Courtney said, "if anyone saw us right now, they might think we're a thing."

"Please. They already think we're a thing. We've taken up living together."

Courtney laughed and caught herself, as her shoulder didn't enjoy the mirth.

"When you're ready," Courtney said. "It's not far. Just don't drop the torch."

"Ready," Brianna said.

Courtney picked up her knife and, together, she and Brianna shuffled across the kitchen floor. While the table wasn't far away, it seemed like a mile. Courtney's skin began to itch again. The puncture wounds were like four little mouths, pulsing with pain. She wondered if her shoulder would ever be the same. They reached the table, and Brianna plopped into a chair. She laid down the torch and gripped the table with both hands.

"Vodka with your medication?" Courtney asked.

"You had to ask?"

"Don't move."

Brianna's chuckle was short-lived.

Courtney made her way to the vodka bottle. There was a glass on the table, and that was all she needed. She set the bottle on the table and looked about.

"Where did it go?"

"What?" Brianna asked.

"The first-aid bag. I brought it down and put in on the table, and now, it's gone."

"The bloke took it."

"Why?"

"Because it might help us."

Brianna held out her hand, and Courtney poured two fingers of vodka into the glass, before she handed it over. Courtney watched, as Brianna took the vodka in two gulps. Then, Courtney repeated the operation and downed her own vodka.

"I don't think I can move," Brianna said. "The world is made of swirling lights and tilting walls."

"I understand." Courtney spotted her purse across the room. "I'm going to get my phone and call for help. You will be all right?"

"I'll be fine. The vodka is quite warm, isn't it."

Courtney poured a little more into the glass and pushed it to Brianna.

"Sip it," Courtney said.

"I intend to. Go."

Courtney left the light on the table. Holding her arm to keep her shoulder from bouncing, she managed to reach her purse. To her surprise, her phone was inside.

"He forgot," Courtney said.

"Forgot what?"

"To steal my phone. Now, we'll get the bloody Bobbies and put this bloke in jail."

Courtney pulled out her phone and immediately dialled emergency services.

And got nothing.

CHAPTER TEN

"That can't be."

"What can't be?"

"My phone won't work."

"Power? Connections?"

Courtney looked at her screen. "Power. No connectivity."

"I thought you said this house was a hot spot."

"It was." Courtney thought a moment. "And that's it."

"You keep saying that, but I'm not so sure you know what you're doing."

"When the power went out, the computer and router and everything died. Unfortunately, they cannot restart themselves."

"That means?"

"I have to reboot them."

"Where are they?"

"Upstairs in my bedroom."

"Why are they there?"

"Because, I thought I might work at night, and well, it was easier to put them there."

"You're leaving me?"

Courtney heard the fear in Brianna's voice.

"I don't want to, but I need to reset the electronics. And you are in no condition to climb stairs."

"You can't leave me. The ghost is around, and it's dangerous. It might kill me."

"If the bloke, and it is a bloke, wanted to kill you, he would have done it already. After all, you were just lying there."

"Just because it spared me once, doesn't mean the ghost will spare me twice."

Courtney looked around. Then, she grabbed a chair and set it against the wall.

"Sit here," Courtney said. "Hold on to your knife. With your back to the wall, not even a ghost can get to you without you cutting them."

Brianna's face twisted, and Courtney knew Brianna was about to cry.

"Don't, Brianna, don't. Hold yourself together. Five minutes, five minutes is all I need. The router will be up, and I'll call the police. You can certainly protect yourself for five minutes."

Courtney gently pulled Brianna out of her seat, although the effort sent pain pulsing through Courtney's shoulder. Brianna managed to lower herself onto the chair. Courtney handed Brianna a knife.

"All right?" Courtney asked.

"Glass." Brianna pointed.

Courtney added more vodka to the glass before she handed it to Brianna.

"If someone appears, scream," Courtney said. "Scream as loud as you can. I'll come running, no matter what."

"You won't leave me?"

"No, I'll be right back." Courtney started to leave and came back. She plucked the torch off the table and headed out.

"What will I use?" Brianna asked.

"Where is your phone?" Courtney asked.

Brianna frowned, trying to remember. "I...I don't know."

"Never mind." Courtney thought a moment and handed the torch to Brianna. "I'll use the torch app on my phone, if I need it. You hang onto the torch."

"Thank you." Brianna was genuinely relieved.

"Remember. Scream."

Brianna rested her head against the wall. "I'll remember."

Courtney squeezed Brianna's shoulder. "And stay awake."

"I don't think there is any way I can sleep at this point."

With that, Courtney hurried from the kitchen, although she didn't move as fast as she would have liked. She limped, her shoulder aching, her skin crawling. Phone in one hand, knife in the other, she mounted the stairs to the second floor. While she was mindful, she found herself looking down at her feet, instead of scanning ahead. That was foolish. She pushed on. She entered the hall, looked ahead, and stopped.

A haze had formed in the hall, almost a fog, which made Courtney rub her eyes. The problem had to be in her eyes, didn't it? Fogs didn't appear inside houses. Even as she stared, the fog deepened and changed colour. It was no longer white, but grey, and the grey was darkening right before her eyes.

She gaped, unable to even move. The fog went from gunmetal grey to semi-black, and as it did, it seemed roil in front of her. Like some computer-generated graphic in a horror movie, the hall was suddenly filled with blackening clouds that festered with menace.

Worse, they waited between her and her bedroom...the electronics.

Fear danced inside her brain. What was happening couldn't be happening. There wasn't any phenomenon she knew about that could produce what she was seeing. That led her mind to conclude that she wasn't really seeing it. The black, swirling fog was a hallucination. It wasn't real. It couldn't be real. She imagined it, and since she imagined it, she could un-imagine it, couldn't she? She stared. Even as she did, the bloke appeared.

Only, it wasn't the bloke.

It was an ebon shape in the fog, something without a face. The silhouette was part of the fog and yet not part of it.

Inside but not there, not really. It was all part of her ailing brain. Had she had too much vodka? Was there something terribly wrong with the manor house? Some gas that caused her to see what couldn't be? She closed her eyes and slowly counted to ten, knowing that when she opened her eyes, the fog and figure would be gone.

"Nine, ten."

She opened her eyes.

The fog was there. The silhouette was there.

Courtney's lips quivered. The knife shivered in her hand. She fought the urge to scream and run. She couldn't do that. She had to reach her bedroom, the computer. She had to.

But how?

"Who are you?" she asked.

CACKLE.

She jumped. Her shoulder suddenly flared with pain. The puncture wounds burned. Her skin felt as if it was curling up on itself. Her stomach knotted. For a moment, she thought she would vomit, as the knot twisted inside. She managed to stave off the retching, but she knew it hadn't been overcome, just swallowed for the moment.

She took deep breaths, fighting her own body. She bit the inside of her mouth. The pain calmed her bit, because it was pain she had caused. It didn't come from the fog or the silhouette. Her pain was real. For a moment, she forgot the other pains. She forgot her own fear. She knew what had to be done. There was only one way, and it was through the illusion in front of her.

"It isn't there," she whispered. "It isn't there. I simply have to keep moving. It isn't there. It can't hurt me. All I need to do is move. It's not there."

Panting, she activated the phone's torch app. A bright light appeared, and that light spoke to her. It assured her that she was going to be all right.

She took her first tentative step toward the maelstrom ahead.

CHAPTER ELEVEN

Courtney expected the fog to vanish. After all, she had a phone-torch, and she didn't believe fogs could exist inside the house. Instead, the fog deepened. The ebony silhouette appeared more solid. She gripped and regripped her knife. If she had to fight, she would.

The first rays of light hit the fog and were swallowed. No light appeared inside the fog. Nothing touched the silhouette. Courtney couldn't believe the fog ate light and reflected nothing back. She stopped a foot from the fog and stared. It was like some force field that wouldn't yield. She stared, her hands shaking. She reached out with the knife. The blade slipped into the fog easily enough. As it did, it disappeared.

What?

She pulled out the knife, and the blade was intact. Then, she reinserted the knife. The blade vanished. For a long moment, Courtney simply stood and stared. The knife blade should have shown up inside the fog.

That it didn't baffled her. She pulled out the knife a second time. It was still intact. Then, she thrust the entire knife and her hand into the fog.

Her hand disappeared.

An intense cold attacked her skin.

Pain flared in her shoulder.

Her puncture wounds deepened, heading for bone.

Courtney jerked out her hand and stared at it. The cold was gone. The puncture wounds sent no messages to her brain. She gaped. What in bloody hell was going on? Shaking, she pushed her phone and the torchlight into the fog.

Like the knife, the phone and torchlight disappeared. Her fingers felt frozen. A thousand bugs darted over her skin. Terror jumped about inside her head. The fog was so, so wrong. It couldn't do what it was doing. She pulled out the phone. On this side of the fog, everything was fine. But once, inside the fog, nothing was normal. Nothing was right. She backed up a step. She needed to think.

The first imperative that popped into her head was that she needed to get through the fog that kept her from her computer and connectivity with the outside world. She didn't have a choice about that. And she needed to do it, despite the aches and pains.

The second imperative was the need to banish the fog from her mind, as she was certain it was an artifact concocted by her topsy-turvy mind. It couldn't be real, so it wasn't real. If it wasn't real, she could simply walk through it. Simple and elegant. But how was she to accomplish that mission?

She blinked several times, trying to get her faculties to work. There had to be a way through, and she needed to find it. Then, it struck her.

All she had to do was close her eyes.

Yes, that would work. Eyes closed, she wouldn't be fooled by her brain, which had to be explanation for the fog. If she kept one hand on the wall, she could slip through all the illusions and end up at her bedroom door. Why hadn't she thought of that before?

She moved closer to the fog, the figure. She put her phone hand on the wall, the knife held in front. If the bloke was in her path, she would be able to defend herself. She tiptoed forward, until the knife hand had once again vanished inside the cold fog. She paused, summoning all the courage she could muster. She told herself to ignore the pain and push on.

It was the only way.

Closing her eyes tight, one hand on the wall, she entered the fog.

Courtney gasped as the intense cold struck her. It was as if she had slid into some kind of deep freeze. Her nose immediately began to run. Her fingers complained. She wanted to open her eyes and discover what was causing the cold, but she couldn't. To open her eyes was to subject them to a cold that made her shiver. She gritted her teeth and commanded herself to keep going. The knife bobbed in front of her, as feeling abandoned her fingers. She shuffled as fast as she dared, a blind woman at the north pole.

Then, it struck her.

How did she know the fog would stop before she reached her bedroom door? What if the door was in the middle of the fog? What if she made her way through, only to find that she had passed by the door? Blind, she had no way of knowing. She had to open her eyes, didn't she? She needed to know when she reached the bedroom.

And she couldn't stop.

"Shoot," she said through clenched teeth. "Bloody hell."

She opened her eyes and saw…nothing.

The darkness inside the fog was almost complete. She could see a little bit. If she moved toward the wall, she could see her phone and its feeble torch. That was all. Ahead, the figure had disappeared. She took that as a good thing. Now, she needed to find her bedroom.

Which side of the hall?

She hadn't thought about that before she plunged into the soup. Since she couldn't see both sides of the hall, she could miss the door.

Which side?

She wished she could pause and consider, but the cold made her joints ache. She was certain she wouldn't hold onto phone or knife for long.

Left, or right?

Replaying previous days inside her head, she determined that she had done it correctly. The bedroom door was on the phone-side.

She wouldn't pass by it in the miasma around her.

Move.

She kept moving, slowly, painfully. She wanted to wave her arms and generate some heat, but she didn't dare. Without contact with the wall, without that bobbing knife, she was helpless inside a fog of her own making.

No, she hadn't conjured up the fog. This was all part of some elaborate dream. That was the real solution. She was locked inside a horrible dream, because she…had to be. The fog couldn't exist inside the house. Therefore, she was dreaming. She wanted to laugh. She had heard of people who could control their dreams, who sort of stepped outside the dream to study it. That was what she was doing.

In a dream.

No need to worry. She would wake up soon. Then, the fog and cold and pain would blow apart like a playground soap bubble. As soon as…

The phone hand found a door.

Courtney bit her lip. She turned to door, shifted the knife to her phone hand, and grabbed a doorknob that felt like ice. She managed to twist the knob and throw the door open. Without thinking, she stepped inside and slammed the door shut.

The cold was gone.

The fog was gone.

She looked across the room.

And knew she never should have entered.

CHAPTER TWELVE

The bloke stood by the window. He was dressed in a dated black suit, complete with ruffled shirt, and narrow black tie. Long, lank hair hung over his ears. A narrow moustache completed a portrait of someone from another century. He stared at her with the blackest eyes Courtney had ever seen. They were pools of night, deep and unreflecting. And she couldn't help but stare back. His eyes mesmerized her, stopping her in her tracks and robbing her of all energy. She felt that if he asked her to crawl, she would do it.

"Who…"

Courtney had barely uttered the word before the bloke vanished.

She gaped. What had become of the man? What had happened to the eyes that stole her very will? One moment, he was there, as menacing as a snake. The next, he was gone. She was alone in the large room, her phone torch shining, her knife ready. She spun, looking for him, as if she had moved without her noticing.

She was alone. The big bed, with its striped canopy, stood unmarred. The heavy bureau and armoire looked back at her. The mirror reflected no one but her. The windows were filled with night.

Where had he gone?

She shook. She was no longer certain the bloke had been there at all. Her mind had manufactured a villain, just as it had conjured up the fog. She was imagining the worst things possible. The bloke was a stereotype, a made-for-telly baddie she had seen before. That was the truth of the matter. And while he was an evil omen, he was nothing compared to her ailing brain.

She had fallen over the edge and was quickly descending into madness. She shook her head and immediately regretted it. Pain surged through her body. Her skin burned. She closed her eyes and bit her lip and waited for the pain to ebb. When it did, she opened her eyes and spotted the desk with its computer and router, all dark and in need of rebooting. Panting, she limped across the room.

The devices started with their assortment of lights and beeps. The familiar sounds soothed her a little. She extinguished the torch app and sat. Relief flooded her. She couldn't remember a chair so welcome. She had the notion that if she were alone, she would limp to the bed and sleep. But she wasn't alone.

She had stupid Brianna with her. Brianna, who was virtually useless on a night like this. No doubt, Brianna had already passed out from the vodka, her head on the table, drooling like some three year old.

Courtney had a good mind to just leave Brianna alone with her vodka and drool. Yes, that made sense. Why try to help such a worthless creature. A dog would make a better companion. As soon as the devices came alive, Courtney was going to rest for a moment, a little nap, something she needed far more than a snivelling woman like Brianna. Let the simp fend for herself. That was the way of the world, wasn't it? The bloke could have her.

On the screen, Courtney's email beeped and showed a number of unread messages. She stared for a moment, before she blinked, suddenly realizing what she had been thinking.

"Oh, my god," Courtney said out loud. "Brianna."

Courtney immediately opened her browser, looking for a way to contact the Bobbies. She smiled as the official police site popped onto the screen. The emergency call was right in front of her. One click, and they would be on their way. She grabbed the mouse.

Everything went dark.

She stared a moment, before the lament escaped her lips.

"NOOOOOOOOOOOOOOOOOOO."

She picked up the mouse and slammed it on the desk.

She pushed the computer's on/off button.

She grabbed the router and shook it.

Nothing. Nothing worked. There was no power. In the eerie, scant light, she waited, hoping that the electricity would begin to flow again. It didn't.

Fingers danced across the back of her neck.

Courtney SCREAMED.

In her scurry to get away, Courtney knocked over the chair and hit the floor hard, her shoulder exploding in pain, her breath stopped for the moment. She grabbed her shoulder and held it, even as tears filled her eyes.

"Noooo," Courtney sobbed. "Oh, god, no."

CACKLE

The bloke's cackle reminded Courtney that she was still in grave danger. Still crying, she pushed herself to her knees. She looked about, but she knew she wouldn't be able to find the man in black. His oily eyes had no sheen. He could be anywhere. She squeezed her hand, only to find that she no longer held the knife. Where...?

On the desk, with her phone. She needed both. She needed the torch. She needed a weapon. She even needed Brianna. The two of them stood a better chance of escaping, right? Together, they could handle the bloke, pain or no pain.

Using one hand, Courtney managed to climb back onto the chair. Looking over her shoulder, she felt across the desktop, until her hand found the phone. She pulled it to her, as a starving woman would rake in a three-day-old slice of bread. The phone was salvation.

She flipped it over, activated the screen, and tapped the torch app. The light appeared, and she giggled like a madwoman. The light was like an opiate to an addict. She snatched up the phone and shone the light all about.

She was alone.

As alone as the light allowed.

She picked up the knife with her bad arm, and that would have to do. Her shoulder complained. She ignored it the best she could. She wondered what she should do next. But that was foolish. She knew. She had to find the master electrical box in the basement. That was the only way to ensure that the lights would come on and stay on.

The basement.

The dungeon.

The mere thought of going there made Courtney shake. But she didn't have a choice. She would gather up Brianna, and, together, they would brave the...dungeon.

She stood and heard the sea breeze keen around the corners of the manor house. The sound was forlorn, a funeral sound. Death stalked the cliff edge. Death was coming for her.

The puncture wounds on her arm flamed with new pain. She battled the urge to climb into bed and pull the covers over her head. There was no safety in the bedroom.

Brianna.

The dungeon.

She turned to the door and limped.

CHAPTER THIRTEEN

Courtney braced herself for the dark fog, the cold, the black silhouette. She pulled open the door.

No fog.

No silhouette.

No cold.

Just darkness.

For a moment, she was too stunned to move. She couldn't figure out where the fog had gone. Where was the cold? Surely, it was waiting for her somewhere. Or, was there something worse in the hall? On the stairs? In the kitchen? What might rise from the depths to assail her? She scratched the puncture wounds without thinking. Shining her phone into the darkness, she limped into the hall. She couldn't help but wonder how Brianna was faring. If Courtney's ordeal was any measure, Brianna was in dire straits.

The darkness yielded grudgingly, as Courtney moved along. At any moment, she expected an assault from the bloke in black, the man with eyes of coal. She steeled herself against a sudden glimpse of him, leering, waiting. She told herself not to scream, not to freeze. She had come to realize that he wasn't real, not corporeal. At least, that's what she wanted to believe. He was her figment, her Courtney-created demon.

She did not yet know how to rid herself of her own fantasy, but she would figure it out sooner or later. She would rid her mind of this...thing. She had to. In the meantime, she had to recruit Brianna and find the main electrical panel.

The switch had to be flipped. She needed power for the devices that would allow her to communicate, that would bring the Bobbies. She no longer thought she could handle things by herself, not even with Brianna's help. She needed the police. They would not subscribe to her mean dream.

She reached the stairs and leaned against the railing. Her breathing felt constrained, as if there were bands around her chest, keeping her from breathing deeply. She sucked in air, without effect. She told herself she was fine, knowing that she lied. Nothing was fine. She was under attack. She needed to get Brianna.

She heard the wind tearing at the windows, as if trying to get inside. The wind meant a storm, the last thing she needed. She had the idea that if things turned too ugly, she and Brianna could leave the manor house and lock themselves inside the car. They might even try to drive away. But not in a storm. They would have to remain in the car, wait out the storm and the darkness.

They wouldn't be able to drive—not far anyway.

Courtney started down the steps. She took them one at a time, her chest hurting with every breath. She leaned against the railing, shining her light, grasping her knife. She knew the knife would be useless against her figment, but the knife gave her courage. She reached the bottom and turned for the kitchen, Brianna.

The way to the kitchen was unblocked. Courtney did not blunder into anything, nothing at all, and that made her wonder about her own brain. What she didn't find, she feared as much as what she had already overcome. Anxiety was the worst, wasn't it?

Fear ballooned inside Courtney. Something was wrong, dreadfully wrong. Why wasn't her figment harassing her? Why was it this easy? After the battle in the upstairs hall, the return to the kitchen should have been painfully difficult. And yet, she was moving uninhibited. That wasn't right, not right at all. It was bloody hell wrong.

Courtney stopped.

If the way was unblocked, then it was the wrong way. That made sense. She should avoid the easy path. She should seek the harder route. That would lead to safety. Any fool could see that. She was doing what the demon inside her head wanted. So, she had to reverse.

She couldn't go to the kitchen. She needed to go away from the kitchen. She needed to leave the house and take refuge in the car. That was the sensible thing. She could expect to run into all manner of difficulties, but that was fine. That was necessary.

Not the kitchen.

Brianna.

The name flashed across her mind.

Brianna.

She couldn't leave Brianna behind, right? That was decidedly not the thing to do. Brianna was sitting in the kitchen, perhaps in some kind stupor, unable to move or communicate. She had taken a blow. Courtney couldn't leave her. That would be tantamount to manslaughter, because no court was going to believe Courtney couldn't save her friend, due to a dark fog and loss of electricity. No one would believe her. She wouldn't believe herself.

Courtney started up again. She would make it fast. She would rouse Brianna and start immediately for the car. If it was raining cats and dogs, she didn't care. Once they were inside the car, they would be safe. That was good enough. Let the hounds of bloody hell be loosed, she didn't care. Inside the vehicle, they would wait out the storm and the dark. They would survive. Morning light would show them the way home.

Even as Courtney approached the kitchen door, her skin once again burned. A million tiny fires pranced across her. From toes to scalp, her body was afire, a slow burn, just enough to make her wish to be out of her own skin. Just enough to make her want to jump into a pool...or maybe over a cliff.

The idea sprang full blown into her head. She could walk out the kitchen door and let the storm take her. If that didn't work, she could plunge off the cliff. Surely, the ocean was cold enough. Yes, yes, yes, that was the obvious solution.

No need to let her skin burn off her bones. Just a little hop and all her troubles would be swept away.

Perhaps, she could persuade Brianna to join her. That would be ducky. Hand in hand, old friends, taking the plunge one last time. Ridding themselves of all cares. No more antique buying and selling. No more auctions. Not even a brand spanking new wind farm. Just the blessed cold of the ocean. Courtney had never considered Brianna life-long mate, but there was no quibble now, not with the fire and the pain. Not with the darkness and the...bloke in black.

Courtney entered the dark kitchen and called. "Brianna? Brianna, we must do something. We must get out of here."

Courtney shined the light on the table.

Brianna was gone.

Courtney gaped. That couldn't be. Brianna was in no condition to move. Where had she gone? Out? Had she made the jump alone? That was hardly cricket. Courtney would have to talk to Brianna about that. Courtney limped to the door and tugged.

Locked.

Courtney tried again.

Still locked.

She frowned. If the door was locked, where was Brianna?

Not at the table.

Not out the door.

Where?

Courtney turned slowly, playing the light along the wall. And, she suddenly realized where Brianna had gone.

The door to the basement, the dungeon, stood wide open.

CHAPTER FOURTEEN

Courtney stared at the black maw created by the open door. She knew, knew that Brianna had passed into the maw and was in the basement, the dungeon. Courtney knew that the black bloke was with Brianna. He had already started some sort of torture, some drip of pain that would turn Brianna's injured brain into mush. In an hour, maybe two, Brianna wouldn't know her own name. She would be blubbering and begging to die. She wouldn't even be able to scream. She would want only the sure freedom that death would bring.

Courtney shone her torch around the kitchen a second time, as if she had missed Brianna on the first pass.

No Brianna.

For a moment, Courtney considered leaving, just abandoning Brianna to her fate. Courtney was no match for the black bloke. Why didn't she just leave? Just climb into the car and drive to the first police station she could find. Call out the Bobbies and let them find Brianna. That made sense. Why risk her own life?

Courtney knew why she couldn't leave.

Brianna would die.

As hard as that was to face, it was the truth. The only way to save Brianna was to go into the basement, the dungeon. Anything less would put Brianna in a grave. Courtney limped to the maw and stopped. Her insides felt like jelly. Her knees quaked. Fear ran rampant through her brain. For the life of her, she didn't want to descend the steps.

"I'm coming," Courtney said, in a quavering voice. "I'm coming."

She took a painful breath and put the knife in her torch hand. The last thing she wanted was to walk down the steps, without holding onto the railing. That sounded like insanity to her.

The steps came one at a time, and she paused after every step to listen. She heard nothing. No cackle, no moaning, nothing. The basement, the dungeon was as silent as a tomb. The only sound in her ears was the rushing of blood through her arteries and veins. She reached the bottom of the steps and stopped.

"Brianna?" Courtney called. "Brianna?"

For a moment, Courtney thought she heard a moan. She stopped breathing and turned her head, seeking sound like some kind of dish.

"Brianna?"

Nothing.

Courtney shivered, as a blast of cold air engulfed her. She knew the cold was unnatural, something conjured up from the bowels of some ungodly realm. If the cold was there at all. She no longer trusted her mind. She stood and tried to remember where the master panel was, which wall. If she could flip the breaker, light would drive off the darkness and give her an advantage. Light would allow her to care for Brianna.

Where was the panel?

She waved her torch about, but the darkness seemed to soak up the light, limiting the torch's usefulness. Guessing which direction was the correct one, Courtney shuffled slowly away from the steps. Even as she did, the door above slammed shut.

She stopped.

She was trapped.

CACKLE.

Courtney's lips quivered. Her hands shook violently. She wanted nothing more than to find a wall, place her back against it, and wait for help. That would do. She would shine the light ahead of her and dare the black bloke to attack. That seemed like a prudent plan. She could do that.

Until the torch gave out.

Because, even as she considered the plan, the phone torch faded. Not much, not a lot, but some. The phone's battery held only so much power, and when that failed...

She didn't want to finish the thought. She needed to find the panel, as quickly as possible. Taking a deep breath, she started again.

Slow, steady, moving the cone of light back and forth, expecting to see the black bloke's face at any moment, fully aware that to spot him was to scream. She wouldn't be able to stop herself, even though she expected the fright.

"Shhhhh," Courtney whispered to herself. "Just move, move, move, move. Shhhhhh. You're all right, all right."

The whispering seemed to help. Her heart slowed. Her chest loosened. It was almost as if there was someone with her, someone with courage and sanity. Someone who wasn't too scared to move.

"Shhhhhh," she continued. "Just a bit father. You're all right. He can't hurt you."

Courtney reached the wall.

No panel.

She wanted to hit the wall, slam the knife into it. Her frustration was complete. Where was the bloody panel? It was supposed to be right there. WHERE WAS IT?

"Shhhhhhh."

She turned left and right, searching for the panel. She had to choose a direction. She knew it was on this wall. But which way? She panted, trying to keep her wits.

"Shhhhhhh."

She turned to the right, telling herself she would walk to the corner. If she didn't come upon the panel, she would turn and come back the other way. One way or another, she was going to find the panel. She shuffled...one step. The fading light bubbled out into the dark.

Step two.

"Shhhhhhh"

She pushed ahead, one slow step after the other. Her brain and heart were slowly edging toward normal. In a few seconds, she would have all the light she needed.

Brianna moaned.

Courtney stopped, but started right back up again. She wouldn't be able to help Brianna until she had light. The dark was the province of the black bloke. Courtney needed light, the brighter, the better. Light would make the room a basement, not a dungeon.

Courtney reached the corner and stomped her foot. No panel. She had turned the wrong way. She turned. She needed to keep going. The panel was ahead. All she needed was the fortitude to keep going. She couldn't allow herself to stop, not now.

"Shhhhhhh."

The light was fainter than ever, but she couldn't change that, so she ignored it. There was enough power to get her to the panel. She was sure of that. Just a few more steps.

Ahead, the light bounced off the grey door of the main panel, which stood ajar. Courtney smiled. Just ahead.

Just before cold fingers grabbed the back of her neck.

CHAPTER FIFTEEN

Courtney SCREAMED.

Courtney PANICKED

Courtney SPUN and STABBED with her knife.

Courtney SLASHED with her knife.

Courtney SHONE the torch at...NOTHING.

Courtney STOPPED.

Tears came to Courtney's eyes, as she stared into the dark. Where was he? Where was the black bloke? She couldn't have missed, could she?

"No, no, no," she cried.

The light dimmed, and a new fear coursed through her veins. If she lost the light...

She didn't finish the thought. She had to reach the main circuit box, but she didn't want to turn her back in any direction.

She was frozen for a moment, before she figured out, she could slide her back along the wall, keeping her eyes faced out, keeping the torch light moving back and forth. The black bloke couldn't get behind her if she kept her back to the wall.

That was the simple truth. She moved slowly, sliding her right foot to the side, before dragging along her left. It was slow going, but it was steady. With every little slide, she felt renewed hope. She was going to reach the panel. She was going to turn on the lights. She was going to get Brianna. They were going to leave. It was that simple. They were going to escape.

Courtney bit her lip. Her heart pounded inside her chest. She had the feeling that if she had one more fright, her heart would explode. She would feel one huge bang of pain and then keel over. She told herself to slow down, to relax.

"Shhhhhh."

The light wavered. The knife bobbed. She slid to the side, back to the wall. She took the opportunity to glance to the side.

The box was almost within reach. One more little slide. She moved, mindful of the black bloke that might jump at her from out of the dark.

Nothing happened.

She reached with her knife hand and felt for the panel door. It was there. She felt the gap. She pushed the door open and waited. The problem hit her square on. She needed to face the panel in order to flip the right breaker. To face the panel, she had to turn her back to the dark, to the black bloke. If she turned her back... Well, she didn't want to turn her back. But she had no choice.

Courtney stood up straight and shined the feeble torch all about. She took a deep breath. She promised herself that it would be but a matter of seconds before the lights were on, mere seconds. Less than ten. Probably three or four. Hardly enough time for the bloke to strike, hardly enough time for those cold fingers to wrap around her throat. Four seconds, probably three. No one was that fast.

"Shhhhhhh"

Her heart thumped like a steam engine inside her chest. She was too young to have it give out, right? She wouldn't just drop, would she?

"Shhhhhh"

"NO!" Courtney yelled, in an effort to throw off the bloke. Then, she spun and shined her light on the panel. There, at the top, the main breaker was flipped the wrong way.

OFF

She could read OFF, and that was WRONG.

She reached for the switch.

Something hit her in the back of the head, knocking her face into the line of breakers, their switches cutting her skin. Dazed, she jerked back. Stars danced in her vision. She staggered back, managing to hang onto the knife and phone but moving in the wrong direction. She needed to flip the main breaker.

Pain flared in her shoulder.

The puncture wounds bubbled with fire.

Her skin wanted to peel itself from her muscles.

She felt warm blood on her cheeks.

Pain erupted in her face.

She stopped and swayed, still woozy from the blow. What had he hit her with? It felt like something more substantial than a fist. A board perhaps? A chair leg? A poker? Did it matter? For a moment, she thought it was terribly important to know what he had used. Why? She didn't know. She was just certain that she needed to know.

The light was pointed at the floor, the feeble light. That was wrong. Her brain told her that much. The bloke wasn't on the floor. The bloke was out there in the dark. She would never find him by looking at the floor. She blinked, even as her senses started to return. Not the floor. She pulled up the light and waved it in front of her.

The bloke wasn't there.

But the panel was.

The panel door was open, and the switches were all there. She was pretty sure several of those switches were not covered with her blood. She was certain that she needed to flip the main breaker. That would be her salvation. She also knew she would have to find a way to flip the switch without taking a blow to the head. One more of those, and she would be gone. The bloke would have them both.

Brianna moaned.

Courtney wanted to say some words of comfort, but it was all she could do to keep her mind working. The panel, the light. She needed the light.

How to do it? How do get light without getting beaned? It wasn't far. It should have been an easy problem to solve. Why couldn't she solve it?

Then, she had an idea.

What she had to do wouldn't be easy, and it certainly might not work, but she had little choice. With knife and failing light, she started to turn, slowly, ever so slowly.

He held the knife and phone in front of her, as she twirled, slowly. And with every little spin, she moved closer to the panel. She had read once that dancers could spin without getting dizzy because they focused on a single point, not the room spinning around them. Would that work?

No, Courtney had no single point to focus on. Instead, she had a light that stuck out away from her chest. That would have to do.

She spun.

She moved.

She prayed she would be able to reach the panel.

And there, almost by magic, the panel appeared in front of her.

She didn't stop spinning. She slowed, focusing on the switches, the main breaker. She turned away from it, knowing that on the next spin, she would flip the switch. It would be so fast, the black bloke wouldn't be able to stop her. One more quarter turn.

Her knife hand hit the switch.

The breaker closed.

The lights came on.

Upstairs.

Light spilled through the open door and down the steps.

But the basement...the dungeon...was still...

Dark.

CACKLE

CHAPTER SIXTEEN

The kitchen provided enough light for Courtney to navigate. Her phone was on its last legs. She shut the panel door and wondered if there was a way to lock it. She didn't see one, and that upset her. She had the feeling that once she turned her back, the bloke would flip the switch again.

She looked at the knife in her hand, and she shoved into the gap between panel door and its frame. It wouldn't stop the bloke, but it might provide her a few precious seconds. Unarmed, she turned from the panel and looked across the basement, the dungeon.

In the gloom, she spotted Brianna lying atop the stone table, that was more altar than table. Brianna wasn't tied in place, but she wasn't moving either. She looked dead already, but Courtney couldn't accept that.

She glanced at the stairs, the warm light from the kitchen beckoning like a lover. She could go that way and get help. She could leave Brianna to the bloke.

Courtney could limp to the car and drive for the Bobbies. That made sense, more sense than Courtney wanted to admit.

But she couldn't leave, not without Brianna.

"Brianna," Courtney called out. "Brianna."

Brianna didn't answer. Courtney frowned, not wanting to leave the panel, not wanting to tempt the darkness to return. Yet, she didn't have a choice. She glanced at her phone. Hardly enough power for what she had to do. And every second dimmed her light.

Every second added to pain of the tine marks, the complaints from her shoulder. What had her father always said? "In for pence, in for a pound." She hadn't realized the total truth of that phrase until now. Courtney was in. She couldn't back out now. Gritting her teeth, she shuffled toward Brianna.

Courtney had taken but a few steps before the black bloke appeared next to the table.

Appeared?

Courtney stopped.

The black bloke was not supposed to "appear". In the half-light of the basement, the dungeon, the bloke should have either been there all along, or walked up, or maybe dropped down, or even risen from the stone floor. He should not have "appeared". That was unnatural, and nature was not something to be mocked.

The bloke smiled, a perfectly awful smile. It was the smile of a viper, something guaranteed to cause great pain, perhaps death.

Like the mouse trapped by the viper's stare, Courtney was frozen. She didn't know if she should proceed or retreat. Fear raced through her veins. Indecision leaped about in her brain. She waved her hand, before she remembered she no longer had her knife.

CACKLE

For a moment, Courtney thought a bit of levity was a good thing. The bloke had a sense of humour? Laughter was never wrong, was it? Then, she realized he mocked her. He wasn't afraid. He had Brianna stretched out on the table that looked like an altar. He had the semi-darkness. He had a…knife.

Courtney noticed the knife in the bloke's hand, the hand hanging at his side. It was Brianna's knife. He had taken it from her. It gleamed slightly, its edge sharp and tantalizing. That was the thing about knives. They always wanted to cut. They were the surgeons of the kitchen, those things that lived to slice and open and bleed.

Yes, bleed. That was their job, to bleed, and they lived for nothing more than a slip, a slide through greasy fingers. Then, they could bite. They could open skin and revel at the red blood that oozed or flowed or spurted. Knives lived for such moments.

The black bloke gripped a knife.

The black bloke waved to Courtney. Not with his knife hand. She supposed that would be too frightening, too evil. He waved with his other, empty hand, as if he posed no danger at all. That was how medieval knights greeted each other, right? Didn't they offer an open hand, as a sign of their good intentions.

Wasn't a handshake nothing more than keeping a knights good, right hand busy? With it firmly in another's grip, the knight couldn't draw a sword or a dirk or grab a mace. Empty hands were a sing of peace.

The empty hand of the black bloke didn't reassure Courtney one iota. And she wondered how her addled brain had jumped from Brianna on an altar to a medieval knight.

Courtney moved.

Wait, she thought, she hadn't intended to move. She hadn't meant to limp one step closer to the altar and Brianna and the bloke in black. She had no conscious memory of ordering herself to move, and she was certain that limping ahead was not some ingrained habit. She was scared to death. She wasn't about to move ahead, and yet...

She moved one more step.

The black bloke's eyes shone with some dark light Courtney didn't recognize. They didn't sparkle, and they didn't gleam. They weren't tinkling like some star. They shined with a blackness she might attribute to oil, dirty oil fresh from a car engine. No, that wasn't quite right. Oil shined because it reflected light. The bloke's eyes shined from some internal source of darkness.

A shiny darkness?

Courtney had never heard of such a thing. Yet, yet, she couldn't bring herself not to look at the eyes, even as she took another limping step farther.

She stopped, shaking, wondering who was in control of her body.

Surely, she was in control, even if it no longer felt like it. The black bloke stood ahead, hand still raised, empty palm to her, proof that he meant no harm. The knife hung by his side, dead and deadly. The glow from its edge like something in a swamp, one of those gassy things that no one could explain. She found her right foot sliding forward, and she stared at it. How did that happen? She distinctly remembered telling herself to stop.

Four feet away.

Courtney blinked. She looked up. The black bloke hadn't moved, hadn't spoken, hadn't changed. She was simply coming to him like some pet answering a whistle. She stared into his eyes. He had mesmerized her? That didn't seem possible, and yet, there she was, next to the grey, stone table nee altar. She stood, staring.

He nodded at Brianna.

Courtney looked down.

Brianna was awake. Her eyes stared at Courtney; eyes that were filled with the fear Courtney felt. Courtney had the feeling that Brianna wanted to talk, to say something, but she couldn't. She was stuck, paralyzed. Her only means of communication were those horror-filled eyes, eyes that pleaded with Courtney.

And Courtney understood.

Brianna needed help desperately. She was unable to fend for herself. Perhaps, the blow on the head had proved too much. Brianna had lapsed into some sort of temporary funk. She needed help, real help. Courtney knew that.

Courtney looked up.

The black bloke smiled, a smile that was both wicked and wanting. It was the smile of the spectator watching the toreador prepare to slay the bull. It was the breathy attention of vicarious participation. Courtney noted the anticipation in his face, the wish for something terribly final.

He held out the knife, the edge glowing brighter in front of her.

She stared. The knife, Brianna's knife spoke without a voice. Courtney knew what the knife wanted. The knife had but one goal—to cut. But the knife couldn't cut on its own. It needed help. It needed a hand to guide and thrust. It needed a will besides its own. It needed...Courtney.

She stared at the knife, and while her brain told her not to reach for it, her hand didn't listen. She watched as her traitorous hand accepted the knife. She watched her numb fingers close around the hilt. She saw the black bloke's hand retreat, leaving the knife with her, that glowing edge that shivered at the thought of cutting.

Courtney looked at Brianna, whose eyes were wide and alarmed. Her pretty face was smooth and placid, but her eyes, those eyes were filled with panic.

Courtney's hand showed Brianna the knife, and Brianna's eyes darted hither and yon, trying somehow to escape the knife that was sure to come. Courtney frowned. Didn't Brianna know that she would never use the knife? That was unthinkable. They were friends, and no knife would come between them. It was that simple.

But it wasn't.

Even as Courtney watched and wondered, the knife slipped along Brianna's blouse. The knife didn't cut. Oh, not yet. The edge slid along the smooth fabric, making a little dent, a little line between Brianna's breasts. Cleavage, that was what it was called, and the knife wanted to create more...cleavage, deep...cleavage.

The knife wanted to see cleavage all the way to Brianna's heart. Yes, that made sense. Brianna wasn't one to be shy about showing a little cleavage. The knife could help her. The knife could make her so much more attractive. Why, even the black bloke would applaud.

Courtney watched, as Brianna shook, shivering at the gentle touch of the knife. Courtney wanted to assure Brianna that nothing would happen. Courtney had control of the knife, didn't she? And she would not allow it to dig out a cleft between Brianna's breasts.

That would be unthinkable. That could never happen. Courtney put down the phone. That hand touched Brianna's cheek, soothed her, made what was coming so much better. Beauty never came easy. That was the message of the knife. If only, Courtney had a scalpel.

"Now," the black bloke hissed.

Courtney looked up. The black bloke stared back, drool running out his lip, as if he could no longer control himself. His eyes, those eyes of dull darkness, drilled into her, probing her mind, her will.

"Now," he repeated.

Courtney looked at Brianna. Courtney looked at her hands. One held the knife, the edge that trembled ever so slightly, like some racehorse in the gate, waiting for the signal to start. Her other hand touched Brianna's cheek. The skin was soft and smooth and pliant. Brianna really was a beautiful woman. How did she manage to keep such skin? Courtney smiled. She knew the pain would be excruciating, but beauty often demanded its modicum of pain. It was all for the greater beauty.

A tear leaked from Brianna's eye.

"Now."

Courtney looked at the tear, that seemed to mar the cheek, the beauty. Without a thought, Courtney wiped away the tear.

Everything changed.

The tear burned her finger, and that pain ripped up her arm. In a nanosecond, it was filling her brain. Agony roared across her mind.

Courtney knew what she had to do.

CHAPTER SEVENTEEN

With more will than she thought she had; Courtney jerked the knife away from Brianna's chest. Even as the knife silently screamed, Courtney pulled back and hurled it at the black bloke.

The knife passed right through...nothing.

The black bloke had disappeared. Courtney was amazed, but she had no time to wonder about what had happened. She grabbed Brianna's arm and pulled her off the table nee altar.

"You have to help," Courtney said.

"Y...yes," Brianna whispered.

Wrapping Brianna's arm over her neck, Courtney supported her friend. "We have to get out of here. Do you understand?"

Brianna nodded, and Courtney started for the steps.

The going was slow, as Brianna was more burden than helper. But Courtney wasn't about to give up. She limped and panted and pulled.

She stared at the light flowing down the steps. That was her goal. She had to get out of the basement, the dungeon. She had to get Brianna out of the house and into the car.

That would be enough for now. There was succour in the car. There was safety. The actual driving away could wait for daylight. For now, the car would be enough. They reached the bottom of the steps. Courtney looked over her shoulder.

The black bloke stood by the electrical panel, and he was struggling to pull loose the jammed knife.

Terror enveloped Courtney. Darkness was her enemy. Darkness was the realm of the black bloke. She would die in the darkness. Brianna would die in the darkness. It was just that simple. Courtney tore her eyes from the bloke.

"Hurry," Courtney managed to say. It was the only word that she could utter. She limped onto the first step, dragging Brianna along.

Courtney's thinking diminished, as she focused only on the next step. She wasn't quite sure how she managed but doing it one little step at a time worked. The light from the kitchen grew stronger. It flooded her feet and shins, like a wave at the beach. She was amazed.

She had never thought of it before, and she couldn't take the time to marvel now. She had to reach the kitchen. That was step one. From there, she could continue to the front door…the car.

The top step came, and Courtney rejoiced.

"We made, Bri, we made it."

Courtney's chortle was cut short, as the lights winked out.

A new fear flowed along her prickly skin. The front door seemed a mile away, especially with Brianna hardly able to contribute to her own flight.

"No, no, no, no, no," Courtney whispered. "Not now."

CACKLE.

Brianna yelped. It was all Courtney could do to keep Briana from falling to the floor.

"Hang on," Courtney said. "Hang on."

Courtney tried to think. The front door was several rooms away, dark rooms, rooms like pitch. In the dark, the black bloke was supreme. Courtney knew that.

She and Brianna would be the blind in a world inhabited by a single, evil man with sight. How far would they get before something was slung at them, a fork or bottle or vase, something. There would be a steady rain of items, all designed to inflict pain and damage.

Could they make it?

Courtney didn't like their chances.

But they had to get out of the house. They had to...

The kitchen door.

The car would be on the other side of the house, but that didn't matter. They could go around. Outside, in the wind off the sea, they would be cold, perhaps wet, but that was better than facing the black bloke. She knew his power was tied to the house, the basement, the dungeon. Outside? It was worth a try.

Feeling that the bloke was ahead, in the dining room or perhaps the study, Courtney did the only thing she could think to do. She turned in the opposite direction, to the other door.

"Whhaaa," Brianna said.

"Shhhhh," Courtney answered. "We have to go this way."

The shuffled across the kitchen was as fast as Courtney could make it, and more tiring than she could believe. When, they reached the cabinets, Brianna managed to put some of her weight there, allowing Courtney to breathe a little easier. Then, as they neared the door that had to be there, the first glass shattered close to their heads.

"Close your eyes," Courtney said, in an attempt to keep glass out. She lowered her gaze staring at feet she could barely make out. Another glass shattered, and she felt the pieces hit her hair. She pulled Brianna along, hoping Brianna's eyes were closed.

Another glass.

Courtney felt a shard rip across her arm, near the puncture wounds. The wounds immediately came alive, searing her muscle. She wanted to stop, but she couldn't. She was close, so close.

The cabinets ended, which meant the door was next. Courtney reached out and fumbled for the doorknob. Even as she found it, cold fingers wrapped around her wrist.

Courtney screamed, fighting the hand that pulled at her hand, trying to force her away from the door.

"NOOOOOOOOO!" Courtney bellowed. Even with the fingers burning on her skin, she jerked open the door.

A blast of sea air encased her, and the cold seemed to knock away the hand. Sensing an opportunity, she grabbed Brianna firmly and lurched out the door, into the cold night.

Courtney too three steps, before she heard the door slam shut. Then, and only then, did feel safe. She let go of Brianna and dropped to the ground. On hands and knees, panting, ready to vomit, pain planted like seeds in her body, she cried. Tears flowed; sobs followed. She had made it. She was...safe.

"We did it," Courtney said. "We did it, Bri."

Courtney looked up. Brianna was not by her side. Courtney looked around and spotted Brianna...heading for the cliff.

Courtney could hardly believe her eyes. She had to do something. Scrambling, half crawling, she managed to get to her feet. Her body didn't want to keep going, but she had no choice.

"BRIANNA!" Courtney yelled above the wind, but she had no idea if she was heard. While Briana dragged one foot along, it still looked as if she would reach the cliff before Courtney could arrive.

"BRIANNA! STOP!"

The stop seemed to work, as Brianna froze.

Only to start up again.

Courtney had closed the gap. Desperate, she launched herself, crashing painfully into Brianna. Both hit the ground and rolled toward the edge. Courtney SCREAMED in pain but managed to grab Brianna's blouse.

They stopped.

Cold, salt air washed over them.

The crash of the waves spoke to Courtney. The waves wanted her. The waves wanted both of them. Courtney held onto Brianna, who didn't move. Courtney climbed to her knees. She looked back at the house. In a third-floor window, someone looked down at her. She knew who it was. She knew what he wanted. She shivered.

Morning sun found Courtney behind the wheel in her car. She blinked and looked over. The passenger seat was empty. Terror raced through her, as she grappled for the door release.

Brianna moaned.

Courtney looked into the back seat, where Brianna was curled up, her head in her hands. Courtney's heart slowed. They were safe, both safe. Now, all she needed was her purse and her keys. Hospital would come after. She slipped out of the car.

"I'll be right back," Courtney said. If Brianna heard it didn't show.

In the light of the day Courtney slunk into the house and retrieved her keys, running full pelt back through the door to car. She started the engine and looked at the house, the third-floor windows. He was there, the black bloke. Even as she stared, he disappeared. She had the feeling that he had retreated to the basement, the dungeon. There, he would wait like a spider on its web, until she returned. When she did, she would not escape.

Courtney put the car in gear and sped away.

If she never went back...

EPILOGUE

Courtney stood to one side, watching the two movers wrestle the armoire out the front door. They were careful not to mar the wood, but she could see that they were having a very difficult time.

"Is everything all right?" Courtney called.

"It's bloody hell," one mover answered. "It's like the thing doesn't want to go."

Courtney could have told him that the piece didn't want to leave, like most of the other pieces she had had removed. The lorries were filled with furniture that appeared reluctant to be carted off. That was too bad. It all had to go.

"Is that the last of it?" Brianna asked.

Courtney turned to Brianna, who didn't smile. In fact, Brianna hadn't smiled much since that night when they both had almost died. Brianna claimed she didn't remember very much, as she had received a hard blow to the head. Courtney guessed Brianna didn't want to remember.

The parts she did remember, she ascribed to a dream. That made much more sense than what had really happened.

"The last of it," Courtney said. "There are a few more boxes to add, but it will all be finished in an hour."

"To think," Brianna said, "the entire manor house boxed, crated, tied down in a lorry, and hauled off to a warehouse. I wonder why we didn't think of that earlier."

"We thought we could work from the house itself. But the electricity proved unreliable. The warehouse will work perfectly well."

The contractor Courtney had hired walked out the front door. As he walked, he wrapped a rag around what appeared to be a bloody hand.

"What happened?" Courtney asked.

"The usual," the contractor said. "I reached into a bloody drawer, and a nail bit me. Someone forgot to hammer it down. Ripped right through my bloody skin."

"There are all sorts of little booby traps in the house, aren't there?" Courtney asked.

"I've never worked a house like it. It's as if the entire house is out to get you."

"Funny, how that works."

"By the way, are you sure you want to leave that table in the basement? We can haul it out, if you like."

"No, no, that stays in the dun...basement," Courtney answered. "It has no real value, right, Bri?"

Brianna nodded. "Not worth the effort to haul it out."

"Whatever you say," the contractor said. "Here comes the last of it."

Courtney watched a stream of six men carry out the last boxes.

"You're certain that's all of it?" Courtney asked.

"If you want, you can make an inspection," the contractor said.

"No, no, I'll take your word for it."

"It seems a shame," the contractor said. "It's a grand old house, and I think it might be liveable, if some money were sunk into it."

"More trouble than it's worth," Courtney said.

"Well, then, I'll be off," the contractor said. "Bloody hand hurts like hell."

"You should get it looked at," Courtney said. "These old houses are filled with all manner of germs."

"I'll look into that."

Courtney watched the contractor walk away.

"I should go too," Brianna said. "The warehouse is full of items I need to put on the market. You'll be all right?"

Courtney nodded, and they hugged.

"Every time I look at it, I get the willies," Brianna said. "I suppose that comes from the injury."

"I'm sure."

Courtney watched Brianna walk to her car. The willies did indeed come with the house. She looked at the third-floor windows. At the end, half hidden in the glare and shadows, she spotted him. The black bloke.

He glared at her, and she smiled. Taking everything to a warehouse had cost her more than she had wanted to pay, but it was worth the extra expense. Her life was worth the extra expense. Besides, emptying the house meant the wind farm could go up that much faster.

Courtney waved to the window, the black bloke.

Then, she turned and waved a second time.

Across the yard, a bulldozer belched diesel smoke into the air. It was ready. The cold, sea air blew past, as Courtney watched. The demolition crew promised to take down the entire house in a day.

Courtney turned to the window. The black bloke's eyes widened with sudden realization. He pounded the window, but she couldn't hear because of the bulldozer. She saw his mouth work, as he said something. She didn't care. She smiled. He slammed the window, breaking it.

The bulldozer bit into the corner of the house.

The black bloke SCREAMED.

She heard the SCREAM over the wind and the bulldozer. The ghost wouldn't be a ghost for long.

Courtney smiled...as the house listed to one side. Soon.

THE END

I hope that you enjoyed this book.

If you are willing to leave a short and honest review for me on Amazon, it will be very much appreciated, as reviews help to get my books noticed.

Have you read this terrific box set yet?

Just 99c/p or FREE with Kindle Unlimited

Find it on Amazon Here

RECEIVE THE HAUNTING OF LILAC HOUSE FREE!

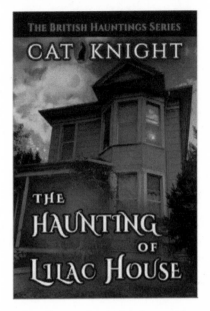

When you subscribe to Cat Knight's newsletter for new release announcements

SUBSCRIBE HERE